Martha

With much love

place of repose

Agnia Mohona

place of repose

A tale of
St Cuthbert's last journey

~

KATHARINE TIERNAN

THE NINGAUI PRESS

Published by The Ningaui Press
1 Pier Maltings, Pier Road
Berwick upon Tweed TD15 1JB, UK

Katharine Tiernan has asserted her moral right
under the Copyright, Designs and Patents Act, 1988,
to be identified as the author of this work.

British Library Cataloguing in Publication Data.
A catalogue record for this book is available from the British Library.

ISBN: 978 0 9926057 0 4

Cover design by Wendy Dawson-Young

Cover photograph courtesy of Adam Ward

Printed and bound in Great Britain by
4Edge Ltd, Hockley. www.4edge.co.uk

Whence it was that the Bishop and those with him who accompanied the holy body of Saint Cuthbert, nowhere found any place of repose, but going forwards and backwards, hither and thither, they fled from before the face of these cruel barbarians.

Simeon's 'History of the Church of Durham' (1096), Chap. XXL

CONTENTS

acknowledgements

I would like to thank Wendy Dawson-Young for her beautiful cover design, Adam Ward for his moving photo of light on Lindisfarne, Judy Kearns-Waddington for her meticulous copy-editing, Lalage Bosanquet for her galvanising comments on the first draft, and Kevin Shearer at Printspot for re-creating a ninth-century map of Northumbria. Most of all I thank my husband Michael, without whom the book would never have happened, for editing, typesetting and production, and for being an ever-patient companion in my explorations of Anglo-Saxon Northumbria.

main characters

Bishop Aedwulf, Abbot Eadred, Bishop Wulfhere and Earl Ricsige are historical figures, as are the three Ragnarsson brothers, Halfden, Ivar and Ubbe, the Danish commander Guthrum-Aethelstan, and the Danish slave Guthred. Simeon of Durham (on whose account the story is based) names four of the monks chosen to bear the Saint's coffin: Hunred, Edmund, Stitheard and Franco. Other characters have names typical of those used in the period.

Aedwulf, Bishop of Lindisfarne
Alric, novice, Lindisfarne
Eadred, Abbot of Carlisle
Beornric, his servant
Trumwin, Abbot of Whithorn
Wulfhere, Archbishop of York

The seven bearers of the Saint
Hunred, leader of the bearers
Edmund, master of the scriptorium
Stitheard, novice
Franco, physician
Leofric, monk
Felgild, monk
Ceolfrith, choir master

Alfred, King of Wessex
Earl Ricsige, Northumbrian rebel leader
Earl Aelberht, his uncle
Roderic, a shipmaster
Aelfwyn, his wife

The heathen
Ivar, Halfden and Ubbe Ragnarsson, commanders of the Danish
    Great Army and kings of York
Guthrum, later Aethelstan, commander of the Wessex campaign,
    and King of East Anglia
Guthred, a Danish slave, kin to the Ragnarssons; later King of York
Aase, a Norse girl
Garth, her father
Eigil, his lord

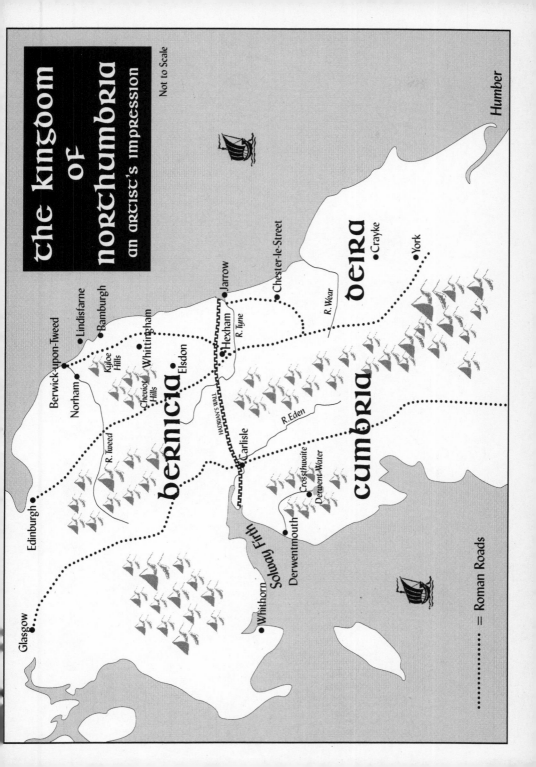

the kingdom
of
northumbria
an artist's impression

Not to Scale

Humber

Glasgow

Edinburgh

Whithorn

Solway Firth

Derwentmouth

Crosthwaite
Derwent-Water

R. Eden

Carlisle

HADRIAN'S WALL

R. Tweed

Norham

Berwick-upon-Tweed

Lindisfarne

Bamburgh

Kyloe Hills

Whittingham

Cheviot Hills

Elsdon

bernicia

Hexham

R. Tyne

Jarrow

Chester-le-Street

R. Wear

cumbria

deira

Crayke

York

•••••• = Roman Roads

1

the starveling

lindisfarne, 871

There beside him were three loaves, unusually white and fine.....
Trembling he said to himself, now I know it was an angel that has
brought bread such as cannot be produced on earth, whiter than the lily,
sweeter than roses, more delicious than honey. Such food, it is obvious,
comes not from our world but from the paradise of joy.

Bede's 'Life of Cuthbert'

HE TAKES HIS SEAT ON THE BENCH. It is November, so it will not be possible to work for long. His hands are cold already, calloused hands with broad fingers that hold the quill as delicately as a girl. He shaves down the tip, trying it against his lip till he is satisfied. At last he dips the quill, props up his copy and starts to form letters. They unroll steadily across the parchment, a straight sturdy trail of Uncial script, line after line, hour after hour. Under the desk his toes twitch and fidget, impatient with the stillness. Still writing, he slides one foot out of its sandal and feels the cold earth of the floor. Then the second slides out and he rubs them together for warmth. When the quill reaches the end of the paragraph he pauses for a moment as he forms a new capital. He looks up to see if he is observed but all the heads are bowed. With a quick malicious flourish he sketches a gargoyle of Alric's head peering out of the top of the B and kicks his companion softly on the shin.

Alric looks up and his grave blue eyes light with laughter. Stitheard adds a pair of frog's legs sticking out of the lower half and both youths shake silently. Suddenly, out of nowhere, Edmund is behind them. His bottle nose is swelling with rage and he brings his rod down with a

1

vicious crack. Stitheard seizes up his hand. The pain sears the nerves all the way to his shoulder. In a panic of pain and anger, he can think only, it is broken – my right hand – he has broken my right hand.

'Heathen churl! Wastrel! May the Saint himself witness ….'

With his left hand, Stitheard crumples the parchment and with one fierce movement hurls it at Edmund's roaring mouth.

The cold from the flagstones in the Bishop's chamber numbs his knees and slowly creeps down his shins. At last Aedwulf enters. He closes the door behind him, unbuckles his cloak and lays it down with such careful attention you might think it the mantle of Christ himself. Then he settles himself on his chair and looks down at Stitheard. His voice is clear as he starts to speak.

'The Lord has put a light in your eyes, my son, and it was not intended for drawing cartoons in His Word.'

Stitheard bows his head.

'You will do penance in the usual way until your hand has healed. Then I am going to move you to the kitchens. We have lost Brother Wilfrid and we need a baker. You will be baking the bread.'

He is aghast. It is worse, much worse than he thought. He has lost his place in the scriptorium. He and Alric are to be separated. Bread! In a flash he understands. Aedwulf is reminding him where he has come from. He is the starveling again, with skinny ribs knocking together, gobbling crusts and stealing scraps. He feels tears rising to his eyes.

Bishop Aedwulf waits for him to compose himself, and to kiss his Episcopal ring to acknowledge the penance. As he waits, he considers the boy's right hand roughly bound with cloth. He gestures Stitheard to come closer.

Stitheard shuffles forward on his knees. The bishop moves forward in his seat till he can lay his hand on the young novice's head, the palm on the smooth tonsure, fingers in the straight blond hair. He starts to say prayers softly, using the rosary with his other hand. The sparrows are noisy in the roof thatch, and an oyster catcher cries 'wheep!

wheep!' as it flies overhead. Nothing else breaks the stillness. Then the hand twitches once or twice. Sensation flushes the forearm, and Stitheard feels his fingers move. The prayers continue, till the beads are finished. Aedwulf lifts his hand, and sits back.

'It will not take long. It will soon be strong again.'

He leans back, reflectively.

'Brother Wilfrid … for bread, of course, strength is needed. Then again, he was not a weak man. Yet the bread – !'

He starts to laugh. His mouth creases with merriment.

'It was so hard! Our poor guests could scarcely get their teeth into it! Even the birds left it!'

At last his mirth subsides and he wipes his eyes.

'Soft bread, my son – we must have soft bread. May the Lord help you.'

Stitheard bends forward and kisses the ring.

The sky is clouded, but a streak of sunlight over the Heugh tells him that Terce must be past and the brothers will be working. He half runs down the slope to the small bay below the monastery. No one is around. The tide is out and the seaweed is stinking. The slow, distant roar of the water steadies him and he breathes in the rank salty air like a purge. Ahead is the tiny turf hump of Hobthrush Isle, left high and dry by the tide. He slips and stumbles over the slimy stones at the low water mark, till he reaches the little island. In its centre is a low circular cell. In spite of the sharp wind he does not go inside, but leans against the low wall. Close now, the sea is deep, deep and darker grey, with sudden glimmers of light making the small waves glitter. A line of gulls pass in a flash of white over the water. On the mainland, he can see threads of smoke rising and the outline of the trees on the side of the hill. Somewhere behind the trees, beyond the hill, is his village, his treacherous father, the people that are no longer his, who have abandoned him here.

'Get up!' Stitheard's father is shaking him. 'Wake up, now!'

It is still dark. He hates being dragged out of sleep, out of dreams and back into the starving world. He fights his father's arm away till Hibald drags him up bodily. His mother catches him to her and kisses him. He tastes her salty tears on his tongue.

'What is it?', he demands.

'Father is taking you for a slave', says Thurstan spitefully.

Hibald knocks him sideways with one hand and claps the other over Stitheard's mouth to smother his yells. He is a free man, from generations of free men, and he does not want anyone in the village to see his shame, though they are not the first. The famine is worse than anyone can remember.

'Me,' thinks Stitheard, slobbering with the leathery hand still over his mouth, 'me because Thurstan is his favourite though he is thick as a door, and selfish and greedy.'

His mother has kept the last of the mildewed grain to make flat bread for their journey.

'Look, Stitheard', she murmurs to him. 'There will be bread every day in the Bishop's hall. You must work hard and one day we will come and fetch you back.'

Then they are gone into the night, the mud thickening round their boots and the cold Spring wind cutting through their famished bodies.

That was five years ago and, try as he will, all he can recall of the village now is the famine winter – the great drifts of snow piled round the huts, too deep in the woods to pass along the tracks, the cattle bellowing for food, the fire in the hut sputtering and smoking with the damp wood, the thin sour soups. After the thaw, the endless rains and the huts waterlogged, clothes wet, boots wet, the baby coughing and retching with the flux.

Arriving at the monastery they are treated kindly and he is given pease pudding and a piece of bread the size of his fist. He cannot eat it all, try as he may. Hibald is taken to see the Bishop.

'How old is the boy?', asks Aedwulf.

'Nine years, my Lord. He is weak now but he will be a good worker when he is fed.'

4

'Hibald, you have brought him as a slave for the monastery lands, since you are our tenant. There is no shame in that, you must do what you can for your family in these hard times. But I must ask you if you will help me in a different way. The Lady Eanfled has given her son Alric to us, after Lord Osred was killed at York. The boy is lonely and your son is of an age with him. I would like to admit Stitheard as a novice, though then his vows would be for life.'

Hibald is bewildered. What will Burghrid say? Her son made into a monk?

Aedwulf sees his confusion.

'Let the boy answer.'

Stitheard is brought to the hall and stood before the Bishop. He will not look at his father.

'Stitheard.'

'Yes, my Lord.'

'Your father has fed and cared for you all your life and your first duty is to him. But now your family is starving and he must do what he can. Will you join us here at the monastery, Stitheard?'

He is astonished that the Bishop should ask his opinion. He thinks of the pease pudding and the bread.

'Will there be bread, Lord?'

'Bread, and more.'

He takes a glance at his father's face and sees his confusion. Aedwulf waits. A long moment holds its breath in Stitheard. It is the first decision he has made.

'I will stay here.'

Now, as he stares out across the Sound, he can still hear that voice within him. That other home is lost for ever, bargained away for a cart full of seed corn and a couple of cows.

The first night in the monastery, and ever since, he sleeps beside Alric in the dormitory above the Chapter. He has never slept in an upper room before, on a wooden floor. There are slit windows in the stone walls, with wooden casements protecting them from the draught. He is given a mattress stuffed with straw and a woollen blanket. A table is set in the centre of the dormitory, with a thick tallow candle on it that burns all through the night. At half past one a bell starts tolling for Matins and the brothers start to rouse. He sits up, wondering what is happening.

'It's all right', says Alric from the bed beside him. 'We don't have to go.'

The two boys listen to the brothers coughing and wheezing as they haul themselves out from under their blankets and go heavy footed down the staircase. Then the room is silent again.

'Are you a thane's son?' asks Alric.

'No.'

'I am. My father was one of the King's thanes. He had a great hall and I had a pony and a spear.'

Stitheard watches the shadows flicker on the thatch as the candle gutters in the draught, and imagines Alric riding past a great hall on his pony.

'Have you got the spear here?'

'No. My mother wouldn't let me bring it. I didn't want to come here. My uncle tried to stop her, he told her my father wanted me to be a warrior. She said I was going to be a different sort of warrior.'

Stitheard is puzzled. 'Do we learn to be warriors here?'

'No. We go to prayers all the time and sit and write Latin. It's boring. Now you're here, though, we can go and practice spear throwing on the beach, we can use sticks. How far can you throw a spear?

'More than a hide', he lies and, to change the subject, he asks, 'What happened to your Father?'

'He rode with King Aella to York, to fight the Danes and drive them out. But the Danes were many more than us – the shield wall broke and a Dane killed my father from behind. He could never have killed him if he had fought him face to face. And they captured King Aella – do you know what they did to him?'

Stitheard shakes his head in response and Alric describes the Blood Eagle ordeal to him till he feels sick. They lie in silence for a while.

Then Alric says, 'Tomorrow after Sext I'll take you up Beblowe Crag and we'll watch out for long ships.'

The brothers come shuffling back up the stairs and the boys are quiet. The straw bed and blanket are like a cosy nest. He can hear the distant surf roaring on the shore and the wind howling outside the casement. He falls deeply into sleep, and does not hear the bell for Prime.

He is still half in a dream on Hobthrush Isle when shouts rouse him. He turns to go and sees Alric on the shore shouting at him; the tide is coming in, he must hurry, he must slip and stumble through the water swirling between the stones to where Alric is waiting, with his arms outstretched for him. He has heard the news and he is crying with indignation for his friend, his brother, and holds him tight to his chest.

The dough is pounded, battered, ravaged, trampled and beaten till the wooden trough creaks for mercy and his sweat glistens on the shiny surface. The loaves form up submissively into neat round rows and vanish on their paddle into the fierce dark heat of the oven. Meantime, their master scowls and grinds mercilessly at the grain, till the meal is fine as dust. Then the air fills with a wonderful fragrance, the oven door is opened in a burst of hot moist sweetness and the bread slides out. It is so high and fine and shining that Stitheard cannot suppress a pang of joy as it is carried out to the Hall.

Abbot Eadred from Carlisle Abbey is visiting the Bishop. He is a tall, heavily built man with a commanding presence and affable manners. Although he is tonsured and wears the habit, he enjoys the extra comfort of a fine wool cloak trimmed with fur around his shoulders. He sits at table and breaks his bread with relish.

'Delicious, Aedwulf – absolutely delicious, dear man. Do tell – who is the baker? Not dear Wilfrid, surely!'

'No. Wilfrid has left us. He feared the Danes, and wanted to pass his old age unmolested.'

'My dear Bishop, you let him go?'

'I would not hold him here against his will.'

'My dear Aedwulf, really we should not let such faint hearts have

7

their way! It will discourage the brethren. You should have let me speak with him. I have sat in council with the Ragnarssons; I can tell you from my heart that they have no quarrel with the church. Why, in York itself they treat Bishop Wulfhere with complete respect.'

'It may be so.'

'It's only a matter of time, Aedwulf. They can see themselves how barbarous their pagan ways appear in civilized society. They will convert, believe me.'

Eadred takes a long drink from the wine beaker and turns his attention back to his dinner. Aedwulf watches, waiting for him to finish. Beside the Abbot's capacious form, the Bishop is a slight, silent figure in his dark robes. He eats sparingly and, in obedience to the rule of Benedict, takes no meat. The Abbot is not troubled by the restraint of his Bishop and does not hide his enjoyment of the meal. He eats with gusto, chewing his meat to the bone and stabbing extra morsels from the table platters. Aedwulf waits in patience till the Abbot has scooped up the last drops of bread and gravy.

'Earl Usulf has died at Bamburgh, Eadred. A fever took him suddenly. His son Ricsige is the new Earl, and he has visited the shrine for the Saint's blessing.'

'Ricsige, is it? Is he a good son of the church?'

'In his own way, God willing. But he has been raised a warrior, like his father, and he and his followers do not love the Danes. He plans to hold a Council at Hexham in February, when the snows are past.'

Aedwulf pauses, and turns a little to look at Eadred directly.

'I would like to send you as my representative, Abbot, if you are willing. You have negotiated with the Ragnarssons and Ricsige can learn from your advice.'

Eadred bows, flattered by Aedwulf's confidence.

'Of course, my lord Bishop, of course – I will be happy to help in any way I can.'

He looks round for a server to refill his beaker. He sees that the Bishop has left his bread and takes it up.

'Excellent bread, my dear Aedwulf. Excellent. An angel must have made it!'

2
Revolt in Deira
Carlisle, February 872

Departing from York the following year, under the command of Ivar (the cruellest of all their dukes) the Danish army invaded East Anglia and first cruelly tormented and then killed the most holy King Edmund. In the meantime, the Northumbrians had expelled out of their province the king appointed by the Danes, Ecgbert, and archbishop Wulfhere, and had appointed as their king a person named Ricsige.

Simeon's 'History', Chap. XXL

THE ROAD TO CARLISLE HAS NEVER SEEMED SO LONG, nor the sight of his monastery's gates so welcome to Abbot Eadred as on this cold February evening. He bids his companions good night, sends for his servant and goes alone to his chamber. The candles are lit, his fur-lined chair is waiting for him, and he sinks into it with unspeakable relief. Here at least he is master; here at least there is sanity. His servant Beornric enters with warmed wine, takes off his boots and tucks up his legs in a blanket.

'God bless you, my son', he sighs.

'Will you eat, Father?'

'What have you got for me? Nothing rich – no meat, Beornric – my stomach is quite disordered from this terrible business.'

'We have a good soup, Father, still warm on the fire.'

'Yes, yes – it will do very well. Bring it to me here – I will see no one tonight.'

When he has eaten, he goes to the cupboard and draws out parchment, quill and ink. The irritation of the previous day is still sharp. The insolence, the folly of Ricsige! His own words were

9

conciliatory, emollient, befitting his position. But Ricsige! – his great brawny frame taking up half the bench, eyes black under his heavy brows, glowering across at him. His mind runs over the exchange like a tongue on a sore tooth.

Eadred had sat patiently in the Council, through all the wild talk and calls for revenge, till he felt the time had come for his intervention.

'My dear lords, let me counsel you against this desperate action. You have suffered injustice, terrible injustice from the Danes. They have taken your lands, they have usurped your rights. But I swear to you on the Holy Cross that the Church will come to your aid, will make lands over to you, will help you to make your homes anew.'

'Church lands, eh?' Black-browed Ricsige laughed in derision and all the battle-hungry young men hooted and cackled with him.

'Abbot, these men don't want the leavings from the tithe land. They want their own land, their birthright and their inheritance. Shall we sit like mewling churchmen blessing our enemies as the Danes eat up our kingdom?'

'My lord Earl, you are moved to anger. But I beg you, think of the good of the Kingdom. Once the Danes have established their colony at York, and the land thereabouts, they will be content. They have no appetite for the North – has not the Great Army gone south to Wessex? If we can but accept the lesser evil for the greater good, the Kingdom will be at peace.'

'The greater good of the monastery of Carlisle, is that, Abbot? Too far for the Danes to bother with, isn't it? You're sitting pretty over there. You and Bishop Wulfhere sit with the Ragnarssons and drink their wine and eat their meat while Saxon thanes all over Deira* are driven off their lands like dogs from their kennels. Some men would call you a traitor, Abbot Eadred.'

What a roar from the thanes! He flushes up again at the recollection. What could he do? He could not stay after such an insult. It was pointless to reason with them. He turns back to his desk, and takes up his quill. It is the last throw.

* The southern province of the Kingdom of Northumbria, with York as its capital. The northern province is Bernicia, with Bamburgh as its capital (see map).

10

Dear Brother in Christ, Aedwulf Bishop of Lindisfarne

Greetings to all our brethren at the blessed Isle.

These tidings come to you by the hand of Beornric. I am newly returned from the Council at Hexham with the Earl Ricsige and many of the thanes of Deira. Alas, notwithstanding my counsels on the blessings and advantages of peace, they are determined upon revolt against King Ecgbert and the Danes. The Ragnarssons are gone to Wessex, and they think themselves secure from vengeance.

Dear brother, I urge you to send some relic of the Saint with an express interdiction against this act of folly and rebellion, which can only bring destruction upon us all. Your words as Bishop will add a greater weight to the cries for peace, now drowned in the bloodthirsty clamour for war.

May the good Lord keep you in health and prosperity,

Eadred, Abbot of Carlisle

As he writes, he thinks of the Ragnarssons. The young warriors at the Council were scarcely more than children at the time of the battle of York and have since grown to manhood during the peace. They have not known the brutality of the Danes. They did not see Aella's torture, they did not hear men scream in agony as their right arms were severed or their tongues torn out. To call him, Eadred, a traitor! He does not sit with Halfden and Ivar Ragnarsson for pleasure. Halfden is a genial man, with a ready laugh and a great love of drinking. But when his face is still, when you catch a glimpse into those pale blue eyes, there is a coldness deep within them to freeze your blood. It is the fury: merciless, loveless, remorseless. If they had known the fury, they would not play at war so lightly.

Weeks later, word comes from Lindisfarne. A carefully bound fragment of Cuthbert's hair was sent to Earl Ricsige, the messenger relates, together with a homily from Bishop Aedwulf. The Earl was at the fortress of Bamburgh and the monks delivering the relic say that already Ricsige lords it like a king in his stronghold. He cast the Bishop's homily into the fire before the monks' eyes but took the relic with great respect. Immediately, he had it sewn into his standard. He has told his men that the Saint is on their side and will ride with them into battle.

Eadred curses his own folly. How could he have played into Ricsige's hands so unguardedly? And yet, how could he have supposed he would show so little respect for the Church, for the most senior clergy of the Kingdom?

There are no more Councils now. Now he must wait and guess and worry. It is sure that even Ricsige in all his arrogance and pride will not attack York directly. Since the invasion, the Danes have taken care to fortify the town on every side and, though the Great Army has gone south, the Ragnarssons have left a strong garrison. It would take a siege of many weeks to starve them out and, indeed, with the Danes in command of the sea, they would have no trouble bringing supplies up the river. Nevertheless, he has taken the precaution of lodging his servant Beornric in Bishop Wulfhere's household at York, to send him word of rumour and gossip in the town.

There is silence as the weeks pass. The primroses and tiny daffodils are showing in the woodland behind the river, and the early mornings are filled with birdsong. The Abbot is restless. His mind wanders as he sits in Chapter listening to Brother Aldfrith read an interminable homily on an obscure saint, or the Prior fretting about unsuitable visitors in the Guest House. It is always the same question: where will Ricsige attack? And how will the Danes react?

At last Abbot Eadred can endure the wait no longer. He announces that he will take a small company of the brothers to Lindisfarne for the celebration of the Saint's feast day on March 20th. Aedwulf, ever the conscientious Bishop, will have been travelling through the countryside giving Lenten sermons and listening to the fears and

12

troubles of the people – he may have heard something…if he will talk, that is. Aedwulf's respect for the confessional is, in Eadred's view, unrealistic.

The feast day is to be celebrated in York also, by the dispensation of the Danes. On the morning of the feast day, Ecgbert, appointed as King of the Saxons by his Danish overlords, is in the King's Hall. He will soon leave for the service in the Minster church and his crown and standard are laid ready for him on the high table. First though, he is inspecting the preparations for the feast. He is punctilious in matters of detail and soon servants are running to and fro carrying out his orders. Halfden Ragnarsson and his kin are far away in Wessex, so there is no one to countermand him. He relishes the taste of his authority. The painted walls of the hall and the long hangings are magnificent, as fine as any palace in the land, he tells himself. There are Danish guards talking in their heathen tongue at the entrance, but that is how it is these days.

Beornric, Abbot Eadred's servant, who is lodged in Bishop Wulfhere's household, arrives to tell him that all is prepared at the church. Ecgbert calls to his attendants to help him make ready. Before they can move, there is a commotion in the street outside that stops everyone in their tracks.

Ecgbert can hear men shouting and running, and the sharp sound of steel blades clashing together. He is astounded. Who would dare to stain the Saint's feast day with such an affray? The Danish guards grab their weapons and make for the door, but they are forced back in. Two or three warriors, armed and dressed in mail and helmets, are pressing in behind them. There is a bright sudden gleam of a sword blade and a shocking thud of flesh as one of the guards falls to the ground. Within moments, there are ten, twenty warriors in the hall, shouting Saxon battle cries as they attack the guards. Ecgbert stands petrified, screaming for his attendants. In the chaos the tables set for the feast are pushed over and benches topple sideways as fighting men back into them. One of the warriors, a tall man with dark eyes beneath his helmet, catches sight of the crown and the standard lying on the high table. He runs forward with a yell of triumph. Ecgbert turns to flee.

A fortnight later, Beornric brings news of the attack to Lindisfarne.

'I do not know what happened to the King, father. I escaped from the back of the hall and ran to warn Bishop Wulfhere. They say the rebels sacked the hall and took the royal seal and the standard and all the King's treasures. More than thirty Danes were killed. There was blood running over the stones in the street.'

Beornric's voice rises with agitation and Bishop Eadred tuts sympathetically. He leans forward to place a hand on his servant's shoulder.

'We will hear more, my son, but first you must have food and rest. You have seen evil deeds, may God forgive them.'

When Beornric has gone, Eadred and Aedwulf sit together on the Bishop's hard benches. Eadred draws his cloak about him. It would, he thinks, be pleasant to light a fire and warm the room.

'This is terrible news, my dear Bishop – terrible news.' He shakes his head. 'These young fools will bring ruin on us all.'

Aedwulf nods and waits, dark eyes vivid in his pale, ascetic face.

'They have killed Danes, in York itself, and they have deposed the King. The Ragnarssons will have to act, no question.' He pauses to angle his toothpick more effectively towards an irritating morsel of gristle left from an earlier meal.

'No question', Aedwulf assents.

'They may attack Bamburgh directly. But it is the strongest fortress in Northumbria and they would lose many men. They will want to surprise them, or look for an easier target.'

He pauses and stares at Aedwulf, to let him draw his own conclusions. But Aedwulf is still, watching him with his bird-bright eyes like a blackbird waiting for a worm. Abbot Eadred shrugs a little.

'Halfden Ragnarsson is a cunning man. He will seek to hurt us however he can. He will surely consider the Saint's shrine.'

He leans back, waiting for Aedwulf's dismay. Instead, the Bishop simply nods.

'I think so too.'

Another pause. How unpredictable Aedwulf is, reflects Eadred. He seldom opposes him, but he is never sure what he is thinking. Eadred leans towards him confidentially, his ample thigh pressing against the Bishop's bony legs. As if prompted, Aedwulf speaks again.

'I will make arrangements for all the treasures of the shrine to be taken to Norham, where they can be more easily secured. However, if I am guided truly, I believe it is the Saint's wish that we should remain on Lindisfarne for the present time. I beg God and the Saint to guide me rightly.'

'They will not strike right away, Aedwulf, in any case. Halfden has taken his men south and he will not want to leave his brother Ubbe in sole command in Wessex. There is time. But would it not be better ...'

'We will stay for the present. If the time comes for our departure I ask your leave to bring the Saint's shrine to Carlisle, for safe-keeping. The land at Carlisle was gifted to the Saint by King Egcfrith, and he founded the Abbey there himself. It is the best place for him to rest – and dear Abbot, you have always been the best of friends to us and a true follower of the Saint.'

Abbot Eadred feels a spring of delight leap up in his heart. His most treasured wish, suddenly given to him, without condition or question! Carlisle to become the sanctuary of the Saint, and, without a doubt, the first monastery in the Kingdom! God is good indeed, and his dear brother Aedwulf! Who would have thought he would let go of his precious Saint like this?

He lurches up with alacrity and hugs Aedwulf with such affection that the Bishop is half crushed in his arms.

'My dear brother – indeed, indeed! What an honour ... what a great honour, and a joy for us! Why yes, yes indeed ... I will order preparations ...'

'You are very good.'

At last they draw apart, shake their robes and clasp each other's hands.

'I cannot tell when it will be, Eadred. It must be when the Saint decides. I will send you a messenger as soon as I know. It may be that we must travel through the hills and, if it is winter by then, it may take some weeks.'

He pauses once again. Eadred considers pleading with him to be more practical but decides not to press his advantage. He is at once rewarded.

'As Bishop, I must care for the see of Lindisfarne, and I must travel among the people. Carlisle is too far. I will appoint you with authority over the Lindisfarne brethren, and over the shrine of the Saint, if God wills.'

3

alric's rings

lindisfarne, april 872

THE MONKS AND THE LAY PEOPLE OF THE ISLAND had grown used
to seeing Stitheard and Alric constantly together. They were like
twins; two blond boys growing into young men. As boys, they did their
lessons together, played together, ate together. When they entered
the novitiate, life went on in the same way and they worked side by
side in the Scriptorium. Their intimacy was as natural as breathing.

Now, it is ruptured and Stitheard is tormented by the distance he
feels between them. Alric the thane's son will be the scholar and will
hold high office in the monastery. He, the churl's son, the starveling,
will work out his days in the kitchens like a dense fool. Nothing Alric
says can console him.

Still they sleep side by side, as they have done since boyhood. But
now, they must keep the Great Silence of the night hours. He sees the
dark form of Alric's body next to him, hears his breath, smells his sweat
– and yet he feels cut off from him by a chasm deeper than the Sound.
When they eat together, he stares across the table at Alric's clear face,
trying to fathom what his mind holds. At last, after Compline they
can walk together in the garden or slip away to the shore. Sometimes,
Alric tells him what happens in the Scriptorium. He admits that he
is struggling, for Stitheard was always the quicker-witted of the two
and relied on his help. 'You are my brains', he says, but Stitheard is
not comforted. What is the point of his brains, if he is to be a churl
all his life?

A few days after the news of the Saint's Day rebellion, Stitheard is
outside, by the oven. The tide is out and he sees a horseman picking
his way across the sands to the Island. He wonders for a moment what
news he brings, before he turns his attention back to the bread, and

17

forgets the horseman in an instant. There are so many visitors now. The upheaval in York has sent ripples running through the Kingdom and men and women come from north and south to the shrine. The Saint will soon be quite worn out, thinks Stitheard grimly.

Alric is not at the midday meal. When he has eaten, Stitheard slips bread into his robe and goes to find him. He hears his voice outside the gates. He swings the gate open. Alric is standing beside the horseman, holding the bridle and speaking urgently with him. The horse is impatient, tossing its head and long black mane, trying to push him away, but he is oblivious. The conversation goes on and on. Stitheard's heart beats so loudly he cannot hear what the two men are saying. He feels he is intruding on secrets he never suspected. He slips back through the gate, retreats to the bakehouse and bawls at the boy grinding meal for no reason at all.

'I am sick', he snarls and stumbles out of the door again, his head whirling. He heads for the church and slumps against a pillar in the shadows, hardly visible to the little clutch of supplicants by the shrine. 'O God,' he says, 'O God, O God.'

For two days Alric is silent, frowning and preoccupied. He tosses and turns on his mattress and spends half the night sitting up, with his head bowed. He says nothing. On the third day, he catches Stitheard's sleeve as they finish Compline.

'I must talk to you. Outside.'

It is dark but the sky is cloudless and a half moon lights the ground. They slip out, down to the shore. The sea is calm and the waves lisp across the sands. Alric takes Stitheard's hand, and holds it for a moment, then releases him.

'A messenger came to me two days ago. My uncle sent him.'

'I saw him', Stitheard admits.

'You saw him? Why didn't you tell me?'

'I didn't know – I thought you didn't want me to know.'

'Only you must know. You, and Bishop Aedwulf.'

'Know what? Tell me what!'

Alric rolls up the sleeve of his habit and Stitheard gives a little cry of amazement. On his arm are three gold arm rings. He pulls one off and hands it to Stitheard. It is thick, heavy gold, glowing and gleaming in the moonlight.

'When a thane's son becomes a man, his Lord gives him rings and the land he is to have. My uncle has sent me my rings. But he tells me that I must fight for my land myself.'

'But you are a novice! You have renounced your land.'

'What he means is, the Danes have taken the land that would have been mine. They have taken the land that belongs to my kinsmen. My kinsmen have joined the rebels and my uncle wants me to join them as well in fighting against the Danes.'

'Join the rebels? Become a warrior? Is he mad? You don't know how to fight. The last time you held a spear you were ten years old!'

He tries to make out Alric's face in the moonlight. Surely he is joking.

'I can learn. I am young enough. Stitheard, it is my people, my kinsfolk. They have never called on me. It was my uncle who let my mother bring me here. But everything has changed now. This is my duty. My father's death will be avenged.'

'I don't know you, Alric. You are like a stranger to me. Is this all it takes, one messenger from your uncle to change everything you have sworn to?'

'Stitheard, please – please understand me. I don't want it. I can't sleep at night for fear. I've gone over it again and again in my mind. I want to be here. I want to be with you. But I can't, I can't now.'

'Your vows – you have taken your vows.'

'Aedwulf will not hold me here against my will. After all, he let Wilfrid go.'

They are both silent. Then a scream of rage bursts out of Stitheard and just as he did when they were boys, he starts to punch and hit Alric as hard as he can. Alric grabs him and wrestles him to the ground and they fight on, grimly, ferociously. The shingle is hard and the stones cut their skin, but they hardly notice. They grunt and struggle, the coarse cloth of their habits strained and tearing, knowing well each other's moves from the intimacy of their boyhood. At last they reach a stalemate of exhaustion and fling away from each other to lie gasping on the stones. When at last they sit up the moon is hanging low over the water.

'That hurt', says Alric, nursing his shoulder.

'Better get used to it.'

They sit together in silence for a long time, watching the moonlight glitter on the sea and listening to the small waves rippling on the stones.

When Stitheard wakes next morning, Alric is gone. As he sits up, he catches his elbow on something hard in the mattress. He pulls out the heavy gold ring, then pushes it back in before anyone can see it. He will get Ceolric the tanner to make a belt, he decides, so he can wear it under his habit. No-one will know of it but him, and he will keep it safe till Alric's return.

4

the fury 1

sacking of tynemouth priory, august 875

From the fury of the Northmen, good Lord deliver us.

Prayer, traditional

Not long after this, Halfden, the King of the Danes, took with him a very large portion of his army; and entering the Tyne with a considerable fleet, he landed at Tynemouth, where he meant to spend the winter; purposing in the spring to pillage the whole of that district lying towards the north of that river, which hitherto had enjoyed peace.

Simeon's 'History', Chap. XXL

'BUT THE CONVENT WAS FORTIFIED', SAYS AEDWULF. He cannot yet take in what he is being told. 'It was fortified! After the last attack a strong palisade was built – and a ditch encircling the entire convent. There were men paid to keep the gate ... surely they cannot have breached it?'

'My lord, they were a great number. It was not an ordinary raiding party. The guards held out against the first of them but more and more ships came into the river mouth and the odds were hopeless. It is said that Halfden Ragnarsson commands them.'

'Why were they not taken to safety?' Aedwulf asked the messenger. 'Why were they left unprotected?'

'When the first ships were seen, my Lord, the gates were barred against them. But they came then in great numbers and surrounded the convent, so that the sisters could not escape. The guards fought bravely but they were outnumbered. Many of them were killed. During

21

the afternoon, the Danes brought brushwood and fired the palisade. We saw the fires. Most of the people of Tynemouth fled, my Lord, but we took the horses through the woods, as close as we dared, to carry the nuns away if they could flee.'

'How many did you carry away?'

'Alas, my Lord, we believe that all are dead. Some may have suffocated with the smoke – we could not tell what happened. Towards nightfall we heard screams, women screaming and men shouting, and flames blazing half the night. In the morning, the fires were out and there were Danish encampments on the promontory.'

'All dead, you say?'

'Alas, my Lord.'

'Osgyth – the Abbess – they did not spare the Abbess?'

'No one, my Lord.'

Aedwulf stares vaguely round the room. He gets up, half staggers towards the window and starts to weep. He stands at the window, holding the wall, and sobs in great gasps. The messenger bows his head, tears starting to his eyes. Everyone knows that Osgyth is Aedwulf's beloved kinswoman.

At last the sobs cease. Aedwulf takes off his Bishop's robe and rips it seam from seam with a harsh tearing rend. He takes ash from the fire and rubs it on his head and face. He dismisses the messenger and orders him to tell Prior Cenred what has happened. He goes to the church, prostrates his body before the high altar and stays there hour upon hour. He can scarcely walk when he rises up, his face haggard with tears.

'How great must be our sins that God sends such a punishment upon us!'

He orders Masses to be said for the Sisters' souls, but gives no further orders. He is constantly at the shrine and no one dares disturb him. At each low tide, more refugees straggle on to the Island fleeing from the Danes. They tell of the heathens raiding the countryside, stealing the harvest and burning huts. It is rumoured that they are making winter quarters at Tynemouth – and worse is to follow.

At last Cenred goes to Aedwulf.

'My lord Bishop – I beg you, there is no time to lose. We must hold Council.'

Aedwulf turns and nods in agreement. He is so close to the Saint's coffin there is barely room for him to stand.

'I am ready. Call the Council after None.'

5

seven bearers

lindisfarne, september 875

It was not permitted to everyone indiscriminately to touch the shrine in which the sacred body was deposited; no, not even the vehicle upon which it was carried. Observing the reverence due to such sanctity, out of the whole number seven were specially selected for this purpose; so that if any matter should require care or repair, no one but these persons should presume to lay their hands upon it.

Simeon's 'History', Chap. XXV

THE MORNING IS CRISP AND CLEAR, with a first frost on the marram grass and a skein of geese overhead. 'We are like the geese', thinks Stitheard, stumbling in the loose sand. 'We are taking flight, like the geese.' His heart lifts with excitement. At last they are moving, after all the turmoil and terror of the last few days on the Island. The tide is already receding and there will be time enough for the crossing, even with this great company.

When the journey is underway, the Saint's coffin will be carried by cart, if the tracks allow. But for the leaving, Bishop Aedwulf has ordered the Saint to be carried with full processional honour.

'We are not creeping away like thieves in the night', he says. 'We will leave with God's praises on our lips.'

So all the brothers at the front are chanting and the altar cross is carried before them. The coffin is borne aloft behind, followed by a long straggle of the lay people, with their carts and possessions and children. 'If we are to die', Stitheard thinks, 'at least we will die all together with the Saint in our midst.' He cannot look around him to look out to sea for the long ships, as everyone does now at every

24

minute, for the coffin sits heavy on his left shoulder and presses against his cheek. He cannot turn his head, or look down, or do anything but keep step with his fellow bearers. They are six, with the seventh to walk ahead and guide them. The sand is wet now, sticky like mud, with sudden soft patches that send the bearers lurching to the side. The coffin shifts on their shoulders and then rights itself. How strange it feels to be so close to the Saint! There is only the wood between the Saint's bones and his. Stitheard's heart beats with unbearable gladness.

'Seven brothers will carry the Saint when we are travelling. It is forbidden to any man else to touch the relics. The brothers chosen are Hunred, Edmund, Leofric, Stitheard ...'

When Stitheard heard his own name he was so shocked, so astounded that he could pay no attention to the remaining three names and had to ask Hunred later.

'Franco, Ceolfrith, Felgild', Hunred tells him. 'Did you hear what else the Bishop told us?'

Stitheard is not sure.

'He said that he had put all the names of the brothers before the Saint, and he believed our names to be chosen by the Saint. We must not take pride from it and we must be prepared to suffer hardship.'

Yes, he had heard that. They must be ready to suffer hardships that could not be foretold, and not to falter.

'Yes, I heard that. And that you are to be the leader of the bearers.'

Hunred nods without commenting. He is a quiet man who seldom expresses an opinion, who never gossips or argues. Better him than Edmund. Whenever Edmund comes into Stitheard's mind, he pushes him out again. He is ready for any hardship, any trial. Except Edmund.

His foot lands in a long trail of wet seaweed which tangles round his boot. He tries to kick it off without rocking the coffin, but it is wrapped fast. Behind him, Leofric grunts at him to keep steady. He will have to keep going till they reach the mainland, and then rest the coffin. He does not care. Nothing matters now. They are leaving the Island and he, Stitheard, has been chosen to be one of the

25

bearers and protectors of the Saint. Everyone will honour him, he will be a Deacon at the least. If only he could tell Alric, his joy would be complete. He feels Alric's ring on the belt against his belly. He pictures his friend's face, grave eyes wide with astonishment at the news, mouth open.

Leofric growls at him again, for he is losing step. The sand is drier now and he crushes small stones and shells beneath his feet. The first straggles of marram grass prick his ankles, and then they are onto firm earth with short, rabbit-cropped grass. They have reached the mainland. Now, they slide the coffin down into the cart and step back, easing their backs and rubbing their shoulders with relief. Hunred nods to them to walk beside the cart as it pulls away up the lane.

The chanting ceases and the long line moves forward faster. They must reach the caves by nightfall. They turn up towards the Kyloe hills, climbing steeply now. The cart is heavy and halfway up the horse must rest. The bearers stand with the cart looking back at the Island. How distant it seems already! – just a thin ribbon of sand and green pasture, set in the shining sea with a wide sky above. They can just make out the monastery buildings and the church. Not a sound, not a curl of smoke rises, as if a strange slumber has overtaken it. It seems like a thing eternal.

At dusk, they reach the summit of the ridge. There are caves in the side of the hillside to the west of the ridge, where the brothers sometimes come for prayer and solitude. A great, grey stone some twenty feet high juts out from the side of the hill, held up by a thin pillar of lesser rock. Beneath is a dry and sheltered sandy chamber with room enough for thirty men to lie. Three other huge stones rest on the hillside outside the cave, giving the place a strange and solemn air. It is said that the First People lived in these caves and that they held their pagan sacrifices on the hillside.

Stitheard and the brothers ease the coffin from the cart and hoist it again onto their shoulders. This action will soon become habitual, but they are clumsy now. They stumble down the slope into the low cave chamber and lay the Saint's coffin on the sandy floor. They rest there for a moment, silent, gazing out over the valley. Remnants of the sunset colour the sky and beyond, on the horizon, are the dark shadows of the Cheviot foothills. The cave faces westwards and the ridge rising up behind them cuts off all sight of the sea.

Stitheard wakes up cold in the night, his bones aching from the hard ground. The elation of the previous day has left him. He sits up quietly so as not to wake the brothers and rubs his legs. How strange it is to be here! How silent it is without the familiar roar of the sea! The night is utterly still and he can feel the breath-stopping bite of the frost. He realizes he has been dreaming – dreaming of the murdered sisters and of Danish warriors with long-nosed helmets and empty, flaming eyes. He shudders and thinks, what if they were to surround us here? Surround us, and slaughter us like cattle? Slice off our heads with their sharp cruel swords, or stick their spears through our ribs? The blood starts to pound in his head and ears as he gasps for breath, till he reminds himself that there are watchmen posted all along the ridge. There would be warning. And it is quiet, so quiet – not even the heathens could slip up the hill without a sound.

He will have to live with this terror, every day, every night, he realizes. They will be defenceless, carrying the Saint. 'God will protect you', the Bishop told them. He hopes the others have stronger faith than him, that their faith will cause God to scatter the heathen who plot against them. Why did he agree to this, he asks himself suddenly. Why did he let himself be blinded with pride at being chosen as a bearer? He is only a novice, the Bishop would let him go. He could go back to his village, he could find his family. He is not certain where it lies but for sure, it is not far away, and the lay people will know. Or he could go and find Alric, he could learn to be a warrior, he could fight the Danes. Surely that would do more good than fleeing over the hills, an easy prey for the heathen hell-fiends. 'I will go', he resolves, 'I will, I will.'

He lies down again to sleep, his mind racing, and dozes fitfully. Habit wakes him at dawn for Prime. He sees some of the others stirring. It is light enough to see the coffin, a dark, watchful presence in the midst of them. Hunred's words come into his mind again: 'He had put the names of the brothers before the Saint, and he believes our names to be chosen by the Saint.' He stares at the coffin. He pulls himself up and, as softly as he can, makes his way over and slumps down on his knees, holding onto the wood with both hands.

'Did you? Did you choose me, Lord? Did you choose me?', he demands. The archangels carved on the side of the coffin gaze at him speechlessly. The wood smells sweet, with a lingering trace of incense. Inside, he imagines the relics of the saint and the fine silken cloth that wraps him. Beside him, he knows, has been laid the Lindisfarne Gospels, the greatest miracle of God's Word ever created.

'Did you choose me?', he persists, and at last there is a rush of tears and he knows that he cannot leave the Saint, that he must carry the burden till it is done.

By dawn, the camp is a bustle of preparation. Everyone is eager to put another day's journey between themselves and the coast. The Bishop will go with his attendants to Norham, where the bishopric is to have its new residence. The Lindisfarne brethren are to be under the rule of Abbot Eadred at Carlisle. The main party of the brothers will go on ahead, while the shrine and the bearers will travel at a slower pace, for Bishop Aedwulf has ordered that the relics be shown at every village and settlement. The lay people will find refuge with kinsfolk, or travel to monastery lands where a spare hide or two can be found. Many of the monks will go with them; in these dark days the Bishop will not hold any man to his vows against his will.

Bishop Aedwulf stands at the side of the track, a slight, dark figure in his robes, blessing each of the brothers and the lay people as they leave, till at last the valley is empty and silent again. The journey has begun.

6

mıracle

whittingham, october 875

*Cuthbert became famous for miracles, for his prayers restored sufferers
from all kinds of disease and affliction. He cured some who were vexed by
unclean spirits not only by laying on of hands, exhorting, and exorcizing
– that is, by actual contact – but even from afar, merely by praying or
predicting their cure, as in the case of the sheriff's wife.*

Bede's 'Life of Cuthbert', Chap. 16

FROM THE KYLOE HILLS, IT IS LITTLE DISTANCE TO THE DEVIL'S
CAUSEWAY, the Roman road that runs straight as an arrow for fifty
miles or more to Corbridge. From there, the Wall Road runs west
to Carlisle. On horseback, if the weather is fair, the journey takes
scarcely a fortnight. But it is too risky to use the road. Halfden will
send his raiding parties far and wide and these roads are well known
to the Danes. It is decided that the bearers must travel through the
hills, over the high ground where the Danes will not trouble to go.

Their guide, Patric, is a hills man and nimble as a goat. He can trot
up the side of a hill without catching his breath and never seems to
tire. He coaxes and bullies his charges all day long.

'Shame on you, brothers – women have more strength in their legs
than you! You've forgotten how to walk with all that praying. How we
are going to get you to Carlisle by Christmas I don't know.'

'Come along! No time to lose! We've got a two-hour march before
noon, we don't want you fainting by the wayside! Boots on and away!'

Stitheard is conscious of nothing but the pain in his shoulders,
the constant longing to lie down and rest. Days pass in a blur of
exhaustion, aching legs and blistered feet; they are all unused to the

long hours of walking. Patric keeps them close to the hills, where the trails are hardly more than a sheep path, and they must leave the cart behind. The coffin seems to be made of lead, and the bearers have not yet found a common stride. They pass along valleys by winding streams, struggle up the high passes, only to descend again into the next endless valley. Each valley has a small settlement or two of families cultivating a few fields along the flat ground by the stream and grazing their sheep on the hill slopes. The people are astonished by the travellers, but bring them barley bread, cheese and sheep's milk, and kneel reverently before the coffin. The harvest is all but finished and they are making ready for winter. Orange berries hang thickly on the rowan trees and flocks of thrushes screech and bicker in the branches. The air is fresh and cold and in the mornings the ground is damp with frost. At night, the brothers sleep two or three together in the churls' cramped, smoky huts, in straw full of fleas and lice.

'Wait till we get to Elsdon!' Patric exhorts them. 'Lord Oswy has a great Hall, and he is famed for his feasts. Oh, you'll eat well when we reach Elsdon, brothers. It'll put new life into you. Why, you'll be skipping along like young lambs in a spring meadow!'

'Hold your tongue, can't you?' snaps Edmund. 'We have enough to think about without hearing your silly prattle all day long!'

Stitheard hears him with a twinge of malice. He must be suffering, he thinks. He has been sitting over his parchments in the Scriptorium for the last twenty years with not an inkpot out of place – and now this!

'You'll thank me for it soon enough, brother! If it weren't for me and my chatter, you'd still be wandering the hills when the snows come and that'd freeze your surly tongue for good', Patric reminds him.

In these small settlements the brothers do not open the coffin, for it is bound with leather now against the damp and will not be unbound until they make a longer stop. But when they rise, the shrine is placed before the village cross, if there is one, so that the people can make their devotions. One morning, in the village of Whittingham where they arrived the previous evening, an old woman is waiting by the cross with a fair-haired youth at her side. He has a slave ring on his leg but he stands erect and dignified. Hunred looks at him doubtfully.

'Blessings on you, Mother. Is he your slave?'

'Yes, Father. I have brought him to pray at the shrine.'

'Is he heathen?'

'He is a Dane, Father, but I have taught him Christian ways.'

'Mother, you are good to him, but he must not come near the shrine.'

'I beg you Father – he takes fits that throw him on the ground, till his teeth lock and he falls unconscious. For sure, there is a devil in him, which only the Saint can cast out. He is a good boy, Father – he serves me honestly, and I dare say if the devil were cast out, he would be a good Christian.'

Hunred is uncertain. He prefers to keep to the rules, but this situation is not clear cut. He knows there are special dispensations when travelling, when lay people can approach the Saint more informally. The woman has faith. He decides it would be wrong to deny her, and beckons her to approach.

She pulls the youth down to his knees beside her and bids him kneel close to the coffin while she prays. His hair is very light, almost white. Stitheard watches curiously. He has seen Danes before, traders bringing their ships into harbour at Lindisfarne, selling furs. But not like this, not living alongside his own people. Anger starts to rise hot inside him. Why don't they kill him, like the heathens killed the Sisters? Why do they let him live? he thinks. He glances at Hunred but his face shows no expression. Then a shudder goes through the Danish youth. He cries out in his own tongue and his body stiffens so that his head jerks upright for a moment. Startled, Hunred moves forward swiftly. He makes the sign of the cross over him and starts to recite prayers. After a few moments the youth slumps sideways onto the ground as if lifeless. Stitheard is seized with a sudden moment of terror, that somehow his murderous thoughts have killed him, have placed the Evil Eye on him and caused his death. He starts forward, but Hunred waves him away.

'Fetch Franco', he orders as he turns back to his prayers.

Stitheard stumbles away to find Franco, relieved to escape.

Franco is the monastery's physician. His father was a thane and his mother a Frankish house-slave. Although he was christened Freodhoric, since childhood he has been known by his nickname, Franco. He has his mother's black hair and olive skin, with a kind but penetrating gaze. When Stitheard finds him, he is standing by a hut, chatting to one of the village folk. He nods and tuts as Stitheard gabbles out his story. He stoops inside the hut for his pack and rummages round for herbs and hands Stitheard a blanket to carry.

When they return, the youth is stirring. Franco goes forward and takes his hand for a moment, then feels his brow. He wraps the blanket round him and turns to the old woman.

'He will be cold now, Mother. We will take him back to your hut and I will give you herbs that he must take when he rouses.'

'Bless you, Father – bless you all. The devil has sprung out of him at the good Father's prayers – I saw it with my own eyes. The Saint has taken pity on him. His name? – It is Guthred, Father, or so he told my son. He was hardly more than a boy when he brought him here.'

The old woman talks on. Hunred nods to Stitheard to help Franco carry him to the hut. Stitheard feels a spasm of revulsion, but obeys. The Danish youth is heavy, like a drunken man. He has an animal stink of sweat and fear. They lay him on the straw and the old woman covers him with a pile of blankets and furs. She brings them ale and bread and leaves them sitting at her table while she hurries off to tell her neighbours.

Stitheard gulps the ale and stares at the Dane. He turns to Franco who sits untroubled beside him. He has been a physician for many years now and he is not easily surprised.

'Is it a miracle, Franco?'

'God be praised, I believe so, in my heart. But it is too soon to tell. He must be without the fits for a few months before we can be sure. We will tell the villagers to send word to us at Carlisle, so that it can be verified.'

'But why him, Franco? Why a Dane? Why did God not save the nuns and yet He heals a heathen Dane?'

Franco hesitates. 'I cannot say, brother – I cannot say. I have been a physician for many years, but I cannot tell who God will heal, or who He will take. We may not tell His purposes.' He pauses again and quotes the prophet Job for his young brother.

'"Shall he that contends with the Almighty instruct Him? He that reproves God, let him answer it."'

After a day of pelting rain, they come to Elsdon. A great semi-circle of hills surround the valley like a bowl and dark piles of low cloud mass above it. As they start the descent, a single ray of sunshine pierces the cloud to light up the valley below and they see the huts and the great Hall distinctly. Cold, sodden and footsore, their spirits lift.

A great fire burns in the centre of the Hall and it is full of people and activity. Lord Oswy has had word of their coming and is present, ready to greet them. He is a big man with a broad chest and a face full of good cheer. Although past his fortieth year, he is clearly still strong and healthy. He bellows out his welcome to them, calling everyone to witness the arrival of the Saint in their midst. What wonderful fellows these brothers are! How courageous! How God will bless them all! He sends servants flying for dry clothing, for wine, for a bowl of good pottage.

'What did I tell you?' cries Patric, as the women come running with fine woollen tunics and cloaks. 'You'll want for nothing here!'

It is late the next night and the feasting has been underway since dusk. Patric thrusts his sharp elbow into Stitheard's ribs.

'Wake up, brother Stitheard! You don't want to miss this! Besides, there's someone here who wants to talk to you!'

Stitheard rouses dreamily and is bewildered for a moment by his surroundings. The bright colours of the walls glow in the torchlight and the flames from the hearth fire throw high, shifting shadows. The long tables are still covered with the remains of the feast and serving women move down the tables, filling flagons of wine and mead. Men and women sit together, laughing and talking.

'Look – the harpist will sing soon and we will hear some fine tales. Not what you'd hear in the monastery, I shouldn't think. And here's Adney waiting to give you a kiss.'

His arm is round a plump, flushed woman whose head covering has slipped askew, letting her hair fall around her face. She giggles, wriggling away from Patric's grasp. Stitheard stares at her.

'What's your name, brother?'

'Brother Stitheard.'

She leans towards him, pouting her full lips.

'Do you want to kiss me?'

He is at once attracted and disgusted. Shaking his head, he turns away from her and is relieved to find Brother Felgild beside him. His grizzled head rests on his arms on the table; he is fast asleep. Stitheard leans against him comfortably, glad of his familiar presence. Felgild is the oldest of the bearers, who often struggles to keep pace and is soon exhausted. No one complains of it, for they know he does all he can to keep going. Stitheard feels a rush of affection now to see him sleeping, well fed and warm. He glances round the hall to find the others.

Edmund and Leofric are together, as usual. Leofric is some years younger than Edmund but he is Edmund's right hand man in the Scriptorium. He is not a talented scribe but Edmund finds him useful. He prepares the parchments, makes up the colours and keeps strict order. Stitheard did not notice his face when the names of the bearers were made known but he is certain his own name will have surprised Leofric. He is looking glum tonight, though Edmund is clearly in good humour. His bottle nose is bright red as he drinks, thumping the table and laughing with his neighbours.

Stitheard can see Hunred and Franco, seated in honour at the high table, where Oswy and his kin, roaring drunk already, are embarking on a drinking contest. The two monks are silent, shrinking back into the shadows. Where is Ceolfrith? He looks round for a few minutes

34

before he sees him, half hidden behind a little group of women. They are clustered around him and he is talking as usual, arms waving, full of excitement. Ceolfrith loves to talk and, after weeks without an audience, the words are tumbling out of him. It will be breathless tales of miracles and marvellous deliverances, strange voyages and visionary dreams. Stitheard loses interest in the scene but remembers Patric's promise of a harpist. He sees the man is starting to play close to the top table but so far the racket is too loud for him to be heard. Suddenly Lord Oswy notices him, puts down his flagon and bellows into the Hall, 'Lend your ears, friends! Sigurd the harpist is here!'

In the sudden quiet, the strange silver notes of the harp ripple through the hall. Sigurd starts to sing a eulogy with elaborate praises for Lord Oswy and his famous Hall, and all the guests thump and bang on the table. Then he sings a lament and the Hall falls silent. It is a lament for a long forgotten battle but it seems to mourn the losses of every heart, and soon there are tears on the women's cheeks. Stitheard feels grief welling up inside him – he can hardly tell from where, till he has to lay his head on the table beside Felgild, and shed tears into his fine new tunic. In spite of the tears, he feels his heart lighten. A new ambition enters him.

7

The Roman
inheritance

carlisle, april 876

Eadred was surnamed Lulisc, from the circumstance of having been educated in the monastery founded a long time previously by Cuthbert himself in Luel*, of which he had now become Abbot.

Simeon's 'History', Chap. XXL

CARLISLE IS A ROMAN TOWN, tucked into a winding loop of the river Eden on the eastern side and protected by the Eden's tributary, the Caldew, to the west. Here, Hadrian's Wall spans the river to complete its passage to the Solway Firth and a second bridge carries the Roman road from north to south.

The Romans left behind two fortresses, one abutting Hadrian's Wall on the north side of the river, and a second, earlier fort on the south side, where the town has now grown up. Both forts are built on the standard Roman rectangular pattern, with stone walls enclosing four or five acres of land. Within the walls of the fort the Romans built their barracks, their granaries and store houses, the commander's house, their administrative buildings – and a bath house, of course.

Long ago the Saxon kings of Northumbria made this fort into a royal residence but, since the Danish conquest, the Great Hall they built within its walls has stood empty. There are still houses, workshops and store houses within the walls but the settlement has spilled out beyond the fort into a small town. Huts straggle away from the fort towards the river, while behind the fort the land slopes gently

* Carlisle.

up towards the Abbey, founded by Saint Cuthbert and generously endowed by the pious King Egcfrith with the estates of the town.

From the Abbey there is a pleasant outlook over the water meadows below, and it is the Abbot's custom to stand outside the gates and admire the view. The river meanders through the plain in long loops of silver water and a spring wind ruffles the shining leaves of the willows. Cattle graze the new grass in the meadows and women are cutting rushes on the river bank. It is his solace, this view. The tranquillity eases the irritations from his soul like a confession.

Today he gazes upon it with a more than usual satisfaction, for the foundation stone has been laid at last for the side chapel where the Saint's relics are to be laid. It has taken three months to find a mason skilled enough for the job, and almost as long to persuade the Lindisfarne brethren of his plans. They cannot let go of the idea that Lindisfarne is their home, is the Saint's home, and that when things settle down they will return there. Nor do they accept his authority, in spite of Aedwulf's express wishes. Well, he, Eadred, has done his best. He has spent hours in Chapter exhorting and cajoling, seeking to inspire some vision in them of the new shrine. Now they must submit.

To Abbot Eadred, the Roman inheritance of Carlisle is no accident. The order and regularity of the town, the great walls and fountains, the mighty bridge over the Eden, bear witness for him to the grandeur of the earlier civilisation, and give a taste of the far greater glories of Rome, the great centre of Christendom. Would that he could set eyes upon the holy city in his lifetime! He dreams of the great basilicas of Rome, with their glowing gold mosaics lit with a thousand candles, their sacred music sung by celestial choirs. In his mind, this is the true purpose of the church: to reflect God's glory in earthly magnificence, to elevate and transport the souls of the believers to a heavenly vision.

Here at Carlisle, he means to start with building the new shrine of the Saint. It will have windows glazed with coloured glass like a glimpse of paradise and walls painted with images of the Saint with Christ in glory. Pilgrims will come from far and wide and the shrine will be filled with treasures. As for the royal hall … he sighs, for it is hard now to imagine a Christian king once again in command of the kingdom.

Still, he tells himself, we are not concerned with earthly powers.

The Spring air is mild and sweet and he decides to walk down to the river. He calls his man Beornric for his cloak and then remembers that the Prior has asked to see him. They can talk by the river, he decides, and bids Beornric summon him. It is probably some quarrel in the Scriptorium, or Stitheard sulking in the bake-house. He knows he ought to move the boy. As one of the bearers he has a right to expect office and respect, and whenever he sees him, Stitheard glowers at him with those strange light eyes of his. If he were a heathen he would worry about the Evil Eye. But what a baker! Surely it is a gift from God.

Eadred has reached the river and is gazing at the waters by the time the Prior hurries down to join him, pulling his cloak about him and frowning a little because this is not customary.

'I was delayed, my Lord. I was with Brother Felgild.'

'Ah – Felgild. How is he? Has there been any improvement?'

'Alas, my lord, he is feeble still. Franco believes the damp and cold of the journey has weakened his lungs. He has a low fever that will not leave him. We can only hope that the summer weather may help him.'

Poor old Felgild, thinks Eadred, staring through the clear waters of the river at a trout flicking to and fro. Aedwulf should never have chosen him. The Prior echoes his thoughts.

'Indeed, my Lord Abbot, there are those who say he should not have been called to undertake so arduous a journey at his stage of life.'

'We must not question the Bishop's decisions, Prior. No doubt he believed it was for the best.'

He pauses, confidentially, unable to contain his observations.

'The Bishop is a good man, Prior – I should even say, a saintly man. But if he has a fault it might be that, in acting upon what he believes to be God's will, he does not always take due consideration of the consequences – of consequences, my dear Prior.'

Then hastily, without letting the Prior respond, he changes the topic.

'So, my dear Prior, you wished to see me.'

'My Lord, we have visitors. They have asked to see you, but I told them you were busy with the ceremonies for the laying of the stone and that I would hear their business.'

Eadred nods.

'It is a strange affair, my Lord. They are the elders from a village in Bernicia named Whittingham. The bearers stayed in the village on their journey here. It seems that a young man was miraculously cured of his fits by the Saint's relics. Brother Hunred instructed the elders to come to the monastery after three months to report if the boy was indeed cured, so that the miracle might be declared.'

'And is it so?'

'It is so, my Lord. But this young man – my Lord, he is a slave, and a Dane.'

Eadred is surprised: a Danish slave is uncommon in itself, since the conquest. Frankish or British perhaps – but not Danish. Where might he have been captured? This was not straightforward.

'We must consider carefully, Prior. Of course, a miracle is always a cause for rejoicing and adds to the Saint's fame and renown. But a Dane, and a slave …'

'They say he was of noble birth among the Danes. He has been baptised, so the elders say.'

'Indeed, indeed. May all his people follow suit, with God's grace. But we must consider, Prior. At this time, to declare such a miracle may cause confusion.'

'It will cause confusion', echoes the Prior.

'The elders – have they spoken with Brother Hunred?'

'No, Father. They are in the Guest House.'

'Good. See to it that they are well looked after, and give them some coins for their pains. There is no need to tell Brother Hunred or the others of their visit.'

He considers for a moment. 'Tell the elders that I rejoice at their news and that, if God wills, I will visit the village myself to see the boy. I would like to see this with my own eyes, Prior, before we make any declaration.'

'Very good, Father.'

The Prior bows and hurries off up the hill. Eadred walks a little longer by the river, till the bell for Terce calls him to worship.

39

8

lecter from
the bishop

carlisle, may 876

The pagan spread themselves over the whole country, and filled all
with blood and grief; they destroyed the churches and the monasteries
far and wide with fire and sword, leaving nothing remaining save the
bare unroofed walls; and so thoroughly did they do their work, that even
our present generation can seldom discover in those places any conclusive
memorial of their ancient dignity.

Simeon's 'History', Chap. XXL

As THE AFTERNOON LIGHT FADES, hooves ring on the wet
cobblestones and sleet hurtles down unseasonably on the horsemen
who gallop along the road beside the Wall. The horses are lathered
with sweat but their riders show them no mercy till they reach the
Roman bridge over the Eden. They slacken off then and let the horses
trot over, flanks heaving, blowing spume and spittle into the wind.
The men have to shout to each other across the sleety wind.

'The Abbey – to the Abbey first! The bells!'

They clatter up the road to the Abbey gate and slide stiffly down
from the exhausted horses, stumbling bow-legged into the monastery.

Hardly a half hour later the bells are clanging all together till the
town is sounding with the din and people are running from their huts
and their workshops, grabbing up children from the floor, dropping
tools, dousing fires. In the church, the psalm is cut short in mid-
breath and the candles left burning on the altar as the brothers run
unceremoniously outside. Everyone is fleeing to the fort.

'Hexham has fallen!' The news passes from mouth to mouth as they run, the sleet stinging their faces. 'The Danes have taken Hexham!'

Within an hour, the four great gates of the fort are swinging shut and an iron bar in turn is slid across to secure them. People crowd into the Great Hall, the stores and workshops, wherever they can find shelter. Rumours move like a contagion till people are worn out with fear.

By the following morning, everyone is sleepless and exhausted. One of the gates is opened and scouts sent out. Everything is just as it always is. The cattle are grazing in the fields, the swifts are shrieking low over the water, the day is bright and still with dew on the meadows. The panic of the previous afternoon seems like a strange nightmare. People start to venture out, going to their homes for bread and onions, exclaiming over the burned pot left on the fire, picking up the scattered tools in the workshop. The first of the scouts return, reporting the road all clear. Eadred gives the order for the monks to return to the monastery and goes to confer with the elders.

For the next day or two, there is an uneasy calm. Watchmen are posted along the Wall and on the bridge and during the day life goes on as normal. At night, everyone returns to the fort and they eat together in the Great Hall or the old barracks, subdued, fearful, listening. The Lindisfarne monks feel once again the terror of the last days on the Island, when every seagull's wail sounded like a Danish war cry. But the Danes do not come and after two days there is news with the arrival of a messenger.

The Danes came up the Tyne in their long ships, he reports. Spies had reported earlier that the Danes were moving north, so the attack was unexpected, although the monks had hidden the Abbey's treasures long before. Some men working near the river had seen the ships and managed to raise the alarm, so most of the monks and townspeople had time to flee. But the Danes had sacked the town, burning the huts and the monastery buildings. The great abbey church of St Wilfrid lay in ruins; they had destroyed the altar and laid fires within that burned so fiercely that part of the stonework had collapsed. They had carried off anything of value, ransacking the stores and granaries, taking captives for slaves. The ships were loaded till they were scarcely clear of the water. Then they returned downstream with their booty, to their camp near Tynemouth. Everything was taken. The people escaped with their lives, but now they would face famine and starvation.

After he has learned the news, Abbot Eadred has his servant Beornric make up a fire in his room, for he feels of a sudden chilled to the bone. He finds himself shivering and his teeth are rattling together. It is the shock, he tells himself. He pulls himself up and goes to the door, sliding the bolt across. It would not do for the Prior or anyone else to see him like this. A deep groan escapes him as he sinks down heavily on his seat, clutching his head in his hands. Dear God! Dear God! He mutters over and over to himself. The so-lovely church at Hexham, so majestic and sublime! Built by St Wilfrid, with the guidance of the Pope himself! The glory of its age! It is unbearable, unbearable to imagine it desecrated, trampled on by the vile feet of the heathen. The time of his novitiate there flashes through his mind – the awe he felt for the brilliance of its treasures, the coloured light that filtered through the stained glass, the miraculous resonance of the chanting in the high clerestory. All gone! Gone forever! It is excruciating, as if some precious part of himself has been mercilessly put to the sword.

Of course, he should have been prepared for it. It was always going to be an easy target for the Danes. Yet something in him had refused to believe that they would do it, could not believe it, any more than if they had wrenched the stars down from the sky and trampled them in the dirt.

There is knocking at the door. He composes his face, steadies his rattling teeth and rises to unbolt it. Now he must be calm, he must show compassion for the unhappy victims, he must send food for them and offer refuge. The brothers must see him unshaken, unfaltering. He opens the door to the Prior.

When the Council meets a week later, the Abbot is resolute. Of course, there was panic when the news came. Of course, the first instinct is to flee. But Carlisle is not Hexham. The town is fortified and easily protected. It cannot be reached from the East by river, so any attack would be by land and easily observed by spies. If any town in Northumbria can hold out against the Danes, it is Carlisle.

Not all the elders are so certain, but what are they to do? It is early summer now, and not many months till harvest. It is too late to sow elsewhere. If they were to leave now, what would they eat? Finally, it is agreed that they should raise the fyrd* and put a regular guard into the fort. They will keep watchmen posted along the Wall forts, so that the alarm can be raised instantly. The fort will be repaired and strengthened, and made ready for siege. The bridge over the river will be fortified with heavy gates. Everyone will be prepared.

The Abbot does not mention his real thoughts, for they are so secret that he has not acknowledged them even to himself, let alone the Council. Yet he cannot rid himself of them and they strengthen his resolution. He believes that Halfden Ragnarsson will remember their dealings, that he will remember Eadred's diplomacy on his behalf. Somewhere deep inside himself he believes that Halfden will leave Carlisle alone for his sake.

Through all the summer and autumn there is peace, though the work goes on to strengthen the town's defences. Messengers come and go. They bring news that the Danes are settled at Tynemouth, that they make raids to the North, in Bernicia and into Strathclyde. Since the raid on Hexham, at the furthest reaches of the Tyne, the Danes have left the west of the kingdom alone. The townsfolk become less fearful, though when the harvest is brought in, they are careful to store the grain within the fort.

* Local militia in Anglo-Saxon shires, in which all freemen were required to serve.

Over the winter months, the weather is often mild enough for work to continue on the Saint's shrine; the brothers celebrate the Christmas feast, and the first anniversary of the Saint's arrival at the monastery. With Spring comes news of Earl Ricsige and his men. They are raiding deep into Deira, destroying Danish settlements near York where the Danes have settled. Certainly, Eadred thinks, it will draw Halfden south.

So when a messenger arrives from Bishop Aedwulf, with a letter that begs him urgently to send the relics away from Carlisle, he is taken by surprise. What can the Bishop be thinking of?

He sends for Hunred.

'The Bishop writes to us from Norham. He sends his greetings to all the brothers.'

Abbot Eadred pauses. The letter seems so unusual, so far-fetched, that he hardly knows how to explain it to Hunred. The man is no fool, he decides, and hands the parchment over to him. Eadred steps back as Hunred reads so that he does not seem to overlook him.

Hunred sees the Bishop's familiar script with emotion. As he reads, he learns that Aedwulf believes that the Saint's relics are in mortal danger and that it is his wish that they be moved from Carlisle. He implores his brother Eadred to move them without delay. Hunred's heart quickens, but he asks simply,

'What do you plan, my lord Abbot?'

'Why, I will try and set the Bishop's mind at rest, Hunred. The Saint is in no danger here, no danger at all. I cannot tell what has put such fears into our Bishop's mind. Of course, he is far away, and it is easy to fall prey to imaginings at such a difficult time.'

A thought strikes him: could it be that Aedwulf is having regrets? Does he want to take the relics back to Norham? Or has he heard something that would impel him to such a contradictory course of action? He takes up the letter again from Hunred and scans it, but there is no mention of Norham, no unexpected news of the Danes.

'To tell you the truth, Hunred, I am surprised – I am baffled even – by the Bishop's request. Have you heard anything, anything at all?'

'No, lord Abbot.'

'Well, Hunred – as you are the head of the bearers, I thought it right to tell you, but there is no need to cause concern by speaking of it to the brothers. I will send word to the Bishop of the arrangements that have been made to fortify the town and to ensure the safety of the relics. I am sure he will be reassured.'

Hunred hesitates for a moment and looks at the Abbot. Eadred meets his gaze. Dark eyes and dark hair too. He recalls hearing that his mother was Pictish, though there is no sign of the fiery Pictish temperament in this silent man. Sure enough, Hunred drops his eyes, bows to the Abbot and withdraws without comment. But later that day as twilight falls and the brothers return to their sleeping quarters, the bearers fall behind the others. Almost invisible in the fading light, they slip down towards the river, along the sandy banks to its tributary stream, the Caldew. They are still there, walking to and fro, as darkness closes in and the first stars shine in the heavens.

9

The Fury II

Carlisle, March 877

THE RIVER EDEN FLOWS WEST FROM CARLISLE for another few loops and turns before its waters open into the Solway Firth, a wide estuary of sand and mudflats where the wild geese feed. From the Firth, it is an easy journey for a good ship across the narrow channel and down the coast of Ireland to the Norse trading colony of Dublin. The Norsemen have been settled there for a generation and, for the most part, keep the peace, for they want trade in the Irish Sea to come and go at will. There is a little wharf on the river at Carlisle and the townsfolk are used to seeing their trading ships come for wool and furs and grain, though none have been seen for many months now.

There is no love lost between the Danes and the Norse. Trade is the wealth of both nations and they compete for the lucrative trade routes and ports. For the Ragnarssons in their new Saxon kingdom, Dublin is a coveted prize. Secure Dublin, and all the trade to the west of the kingdom is theirs, as well as the overland route to York. So it was that while Halfden went north to crush the rebellion in Northumbria, his brother Ivar – called the Boneless – took the remaining warships of the Great Army of the Danes south and west to Ireland. In Dublin, the Norse put up a fierce resistance, the battle being long and bloody. At the end of it, although Ivar lay dead with an axe through his neck, the Danes had possession of the colony. They showed no mercy and the Irish who lived alongside the Norse fled back into the countryside.

Did Ivar's warriors stay in Dublin? When spring came, did it bring a quickening of the blood, the wild thrill to go a-viking? Or did Halfden send orders for them to join the attack on the rebels

46

of Northumbria? No one can tell. All that is certain is that the long ships slid out of Dublin on a calm spring night into the starlit sea and headed eastwards.

A day and a night later, they are coming into the Eden on the tide and before sunrise all the long ships are drawn up on the sandy bank of the river just out of sight of the town.

The monks are in the Abbey church for the dawn office of Prime. After the office, they go to their duties in the monastery buildings. Stitheard and Franco make their way down to the fort to collect some sacks of barley from the granary. Walking down from the Abbey, they see the dark outline of the river in the early morning light and hear the first thrushes singing. They make for the east gate of the fort which is closest to the Abbey and arrive just as the gates are opened. They bid good morning to the man pushing back the gate. He has just risen and is still rubbing the sleep out of his eyes.

The Danes on the river bank wait as they see the first smoke from hut fires curling up into the air, till they see the gates of the fort open and the first loaded cart rolling out of the south gate onto the road. Then they are on the move, half running in spite of their shields, swords and axes, across the meadow to the gate, scores of armed men coming silently out of the dawn light. The two men on the cart gape in horror, jumping down and running back to raise the alarm. One of the Danes sprints ahead to strike them down before they reach the gate. His axe slices open their backs so that the blood spurts out. Their screams are the first warning of the raid.

Inside the fort, the men are taken utterly by surprise. They snatch up their weapons, bellowing the alarm. Some half-dozen run for the south gate, trying to haul the heavy wooden gates closed, but the Danes are already half way in. There is a long moment of heaving and shouting as more men rush forward to close the gates so they can be bolted. It is a deadly game of tug o'war. The gates swing to and fro, almost made fast when a surge from the Danes opens them wide enough for two warriors to squeeze through into the fort. They have silver helmets with long nose pieces, and bright swords in their hands. Each Dane swings his sword once, and two men drop to the ground.

Bright red blood streams out onto the cobbled stones. The defenders fall back and start to run. The gates swing open and scores of Danes pour into the fort.

From the granary at the back of the fort, Stitheard and Franco hear the shouting and hurry to the door. Outside, they see utter confusion. Men and women are running in all directions, shouting to each other, screaming and weeping, dragging children along, running to take cover in the buildings. At the other end of the fort, at the south gate, they can see a glint of metal in the sunlight from the Danes' helmets and bodies lying on the ground. There is a stench of fresh blood as in a slaughterhouse. As the Danes head towards the Great Hall, an axe-wielding Saxon rushes at them, screaming like a madman. The scream stops mid-breath as a Dane runs him through and he falls to the ground like a sack. Another attacker grabs a woman with a baby in her arms. He knocks the infant to the ground, kicks it aside and pulls the woman into a hut. Stitheard starts forward, but Franco pulls him back.

'The east gate!' he shouts above the uproar. 'Go to the church!'

They set off towards the gate but are pushed back by people running towards them, looking behind them in panic, screaming that the Danes are there. Stitheard and Franco glance at each other, panting with fear.

'The north?'

Franco nods and they slip back inside the granary, past the pale musty-smelling piles of grain, to the rear door. As Franco pulls it open, the tumult of noise hits them again. From here, they cannot see the lower end of the fort, only the road leading to the gate. Stitheard glances behind them and sees two Danes come out of a hut and head for the granary door. The first of the killing is over and now they are looking for plunder – plunder and slaves.

'Hurry!' he shouts to Franco. 'They are behind us!'

Tucking up their habits, they start to run for the road. As they reach it, and start to make for the gate, Stitheard looks back again. One of the Danes has decided to come after them. He is not hurrying but his stride is long and fast. Even if they get through the gate, he will soon catch up to them if they cannot hasten.

'Faster!' he screams at Franco. There are others fleeing ahead of them, already through the gate. He grabs Franco's arm, and tows him along as he sprints down the road. Fear drives every muscle and sinew of his body. He is running for his life, and somehow he has got to take his brother, slower and older, with him.

At last they are through the gate, and without a word both of them turn right and start to run up the slope towards the Abbey. Franco is stumbling now, with his breath coming in huge gasps. Stitheard risks a look back. Their pursuer has not followed them through the gate; he must have found easier prey. Franco doubles over, trying to get his breath. 'Dear God', he gasps. 'Dear God.' Stitheard too feels his heart beating so hard it seems close to bursting his chest. But they must keep moving.

'Come, Franco!' he says. 'They'll be at the church soon.' Franco pulls himself up and Stitheard takes his arm up for the last effort up the slope.

When they reach the church, they find the Abbot standing alone outside the entrance, his face chalk white and his eyes starting with panic. When he sees Stitheard and Franco, he runs to meet them, stammering prayers and greetings. He embraces them both, his hands shaking. Behind him, they see Edmund, Leofric, Ceolfrith and Hunred bringing the Saint's coffin out of the church on their shoulders. Felgild is too weak to help and, with only four bearers, they are struggling with the weight. There are shouts of joy, of relief, as they see the other two arrive. Still gasping for breath, Stitheard and Franco slip their shoulders under the coffin. There is a moment of pause as they adjust the weight and settle the coffin evenly.

Below them, smoke rises from the town and flames are starting to leap above the walls of the fort. There is a clamour of men shouting and fighting, of children wailing and women screaming. It is as if the apocalypse has dawned. They have feared this for so long but, now it is upon them, they cannot take in what they see. It is a relief when Hunred gives the word and they start to move. The Abbot clutches at Hunred's sleeve.

'I have sent for horses, for a cart ....'

But Hunred is resolute now. He shakes his head and does not pause. The bearers break into a steady half run, moving away from the church towards the low valley of the Caldew. Felgild catches the Abbot's hands.

'Abbot, they will take the relics to a hiding place. We have arranged it. A horse and cart will be seen, the Danes will take it. You must flee, my lord.'

'I have betrayed the Bishop, Felgild. I must stay with the relics.'

So Felgild takes his hand, and with his staff in the other they stumble after the bearers.

As they move down towards the river, the bearers cannot turn to see if they are pursued, they can only keep moving forward, holding the coffin steady, trying to sense each other's movements. They must think of nothing but the flight. When they reach the Caldew, they plunge into the water without hesitation, but slowly now as it reaches to their thighs. On the far bank, a punt is moored. They wade over to it and lower the coffin into it, gasping and panting for breath. Once untied, they set it into the stream and let it half carry them down towards the Eden.

As the current takes them slowly downstream, the banks begin to rise up steeply on either side, thickly wooded, and soon they are closed in with only the sky above. When a shallow beach of gravel appears on the far side, they push the punt out of the water. Once more they heave together and hoist the coffin up on to their shoulders. They are nearly there. Now it is a final scramble up the bank through the undergrowth and trees, a desperate pushing and shoving till the coffin slips and almost topples off into the bushes. Hidden by the trees, there is a cliff overhanging the river, with space to walk beneath and dry sand. When they reach it, they first lower the coffin to the ground, then fall down beside it themselves, spent with exhaustion. Leofric is the first to speak.

'We should hide the punt.'

He, Ceolfrith and Stitheard struggle back down to the river and start to drag the punt up the bank. It is heavy and awkward as they shove it out of sight behind bushes and trees. Suddenly they hear splashing from the river, a sound of men moving through the water. They shrink behind the trees in terror as two figures come into sight. Is it possible that they could be followed so soon? The figures move very slowly, too slowly for Danes. Are they fugitives like themselves? Then a sudden moment of recognition – it is Felgild, and it is the Abbot! They run down to them and help them from the water, embracing them like lost souls, Leofric scolding Felgild and railing at his wet clothes.

'I had to come, Leofric – the Abbot ordered it.'

He is pale and his breath rasping, but his face is alight. He clasps Leofric tightly.

'I would far sooner die here with all of you than …, than ….'

He half sinks but Leofric keeps him upright while Stitheard catches his other arm.

'A little further to go, brother.'

The Abbot is standing with Ceolfrith, tears streaming down his face. Ceolfrith takes his arm, and they stumble together up the slope to join the brothers.

For a while, exhaustion overtakes all of them. They sit staring into the wood without speaking. They can hear the distant noises of the raid and the breeze is bitter with wood smoke. Every now and then Felgild has a bout of coughing that shakes his bent body painfully. The Abbot holds his head in his hands, unable to control his grief. At last he manages to gather himself to speak.

'My dear brothers – I beg you – I beg you to forgive me. I ha
brought us all into mortal peril through my folly and blindness
the Saint too …'

He drops his head into his hands again, unable to contin
a long silence. Franco puts his hand on the Abbot's sh

'Do not think of it now, Father. God has delivered us, and with His help we will come to safety. Will not the Saint protect us?'

Franco glances towards Hunred. He nods. He pulls himself up and starts the prayers of protection.

'Christ have mercy on us.'
'Lord have mercy on us.'
'Christ have mercy on us. O Christ hear us.'
'O Christ hear us.'
'From our enemies defend us, O Christ.'
'O Christ hear us.'
'Pitifully behold the sorrow of our hearts.'
'O Christ hear us.'
'O Son of David, have mercy upon us.'

They recite the office prayer after prayer, their voices hardly audible, the familiar words steadying them. When they reach the section assigned for the psalm of the day, there is a pause. Ceolfrith puts his hands on the coffin and starts to intone Psalm 79.

O God, the heathen are come into thine inheritance; thy holy temple have they defiled, and made Jerusalem a heap of stones.

The dead bodies of thy servants have they given to be meat unto the fowls of the air; and the flesh of thy saints unto the beasts of the land.

Their blood have they shed like water on every side of Jerusalem; and there was no man to bury them.

We are become an open shame to our enemies, a very scorn and derision unto them that are round about us.

Lord, how long wilt thou be angry; shall thy jealousy burn like fire for ever?

Pour out thy indignation upon the heathen that have not known thee; and upon the kingdoms that have not known your name.

For they have devoured Jacob; and laid waste his dwelling-place.

10

waiting for nightfall

carlisle, march 877

THEY MUST WAIT NOW TILL NIGHTFALL TO MAKE THEIR ESCAPE, and the day's passing seems endless. Above them, clouds drift through the indifferent sky. Small finches flit to and fro in the branches of the trees, twittering and calling to each other. Cold and hungry, the brothers huddle together on the sand in the shelter of the cliff. Hours pass. At last, the sun starts to sink lower, till they cannot see it above the trees. Hunred draws the Abbot aside to confer. When they call the brothers to come close, it is Hunred who speaks, his face tired and drawn.

'We will go as soon as darkness falls, and take the Roman road south.' He pauses. 'The road is not far, but it will be hard to carry the coffin through the woods. We'll float it downstream on the punt to the Eden where the banks are clear. Ceolfrith and Leofric – you take the punt. Felgild – you go with them. The rest of us will make our way through the wood and meet them on the bank.'

There is a murmur of disagreement from Leofric.

'What about Danes on the river? Their ships will be there.'

'They won't travel tonight', says Hunred. 'Why should they hurry? They'll feast and drink.'

'They'll set a guard for the ships. If the ships are downstream they'll see us.'

Hunred pauses. He glances at the Abbot, but Eadred says nothing. 'You are right. Someone must go down to the river and see where the ships are.' Hunred looks round at the brothers. 'Who will go?

'I will.' Stitheard jumps up at once. Anything is better than and waiting.

Hunred nods and embraces him. 'Take care, brother – don't put yourself in danger. You will be able to see the river without leaving the wood. May God protect you.'

It is a relief to move, though Stitheard's heart is pounding. He is stiff and clumsy at first till his body warms and he can tread soundlessly through the trees on the steep bank, making his way downstream to where the Caldew flows out into the greater waters of the Eden.

As the Caldew nears the river, the bank drops away and the tree cover thins out. Stitheard pauses here, reluctant to go further. He can see the dark blue waters of the Eden well enough, and then his eye finds two or three ships, beached upstream near the wharf. He moves round to get a better look and with a sudden shock sees a man below him, hardly a hide away. He flattens himself behind a broad elm and risks another glimpse.

It is a Danish warrior, still wearing his helmet, with his leather jerkin partly cut open. Moving slowly and heavily with fatigue, he is walking down to the water's edge. When he reaches the bank, he lifts off his helmet, revealing long reddish hair, plastered against his skull with sweat. He drops onto one knee and lowers the helmet into the river, draws up water and pours it over his head, letting it run down his face and beard onto his jerkin. He dips it in again and drinks a long draught. Then he lays his helmet on the ground and draws his sword from the scabbard, tugging at it to get it out. It is caked and filthy. He steps down into the water to wash it.

A red stain colours the water as it runs away from the sword. The current moves slowly and the stain spreads out across the ripples. As Stitheard watches, the stain spreads wider and wider, till it seems to fill the river with blood. He stares at the sword, the blade gleaming now as the Dane rubs it clean. A passion for vengeance possesses him like a madness. His chest tightens as his breath comes in short gasps.

Turning, the Dane lays his sword on the bank to dry before he hauls himself up out of the water. As he takes a few steps along the bank, Stitheard sees that he is limping, and feels a savage elation. It will not be hard to kill him. The Dane sits down heavily on the grass, his back to the sword, and unlaces one of his boots. The foot is badly swollen and he grunts with pain as he eases the boot off, engrossed in his injury.

Behind him, Stitheard half crawls, half slides down the slope and out of the cover of the wood, towards the river bank where the sword is lying. He is conscious of nothing but the hammering of his heart beat in his chest. As he moves now across the short-cropped grass, the noise of the water prevents any sound reaching the Dane. Intent on the sword, Stitheard reaches so close that he can see the bands of silver fretwork round the hilt, and he stretches his arm out to grasp it. Then the Dane looks round and is on him in a second, grabbing both his legs and bringing him to the ground. For a moment the breath is knocked out of him. He struggles up to get his hands round the Dane's throat but the man is too quick and strong for him. The Dane pushes his right arm aside, forcing his shoulder to the ground. Then both his hands are on Stitheard's shoulders, pinning him down. They wrestle for a few minutes, grunting and panting. Stitheard smells the man's foul breath close to his face as he struggles to throw him off. Suddenly the Dane lets go and, as Stitheard half rises, strikes him a blow across the jaw with his fist. Stitheard falls back and the Dane hits his face again and again. Blood pours from his nose as he slumps to the ground dazed with pain. The Dane kicks him a couple of times till the pain in his swollen foot makes him stagger sideways. Stitheard heaves himself away along the ground and collapses again. He tastes the blood running into his mouth. From the corner of his eye, he sees a sudden glint of metal as the Dane lifts his sword from the ground. Terror explodes through Stitheard's body and somehow he is on his feet and running for the cover of the wood. The Dane lurches after him, lunging at him with his sword, but the pain in his foot stops him. He bellows curses into the wood, and turns back to the river.

Stitheard falls to the ground under the trees and loses consciousness. When he comes to his senses, it is growing dark. He can hear the sound of the water below him and for a moment he thinks he is back on the shore at Lindisfarne. A blackbird starts its twilight song and, in the silence of the dusk, there is no other sound. He feels the agonising pain in his head and shoulder. Half-conscious, he staggers to his feet, knowing only that he must get back to the brothers.

When he stumbles into the clearing under the cliff, they gather round him talking, questioning, staring at his battered face. He tries to speak, but no words come. His mouth is so swollen it no longer feels like part of him. He catches sight of the coffin and its silent presence draws him over. But they do not leave him in peace, half shouting now, and tugging at him. Hunred gestures for silence.

'Let him be – who knows what has happened. Give silence a while, let him find himself. Franco – you sit with him.'

Then it is quiet and the men all sit huddled together, almost in darkness now. Franco brings water up to bathe his head, slopping it gently here and there. Stitheard hears Franco's kind voice beside him, but it does not reach the silence inside his head. He slips further and further away into its depths.

Then they are talking again, and everyone gets up, pulling him to his feet as well. They lift the coffin and shove him into his place. As he feels the familiar weight on his shoulder he knows what he has to do, and he moves forward with the others, slipping and stumbling in the darkness down the bank. They haul the punt into the water again and ease the coffin into it. Leofric crouches at the front with the mooring rope and Ceolfrith takes the pole at the back, with Felgild squeezed in beside the shrine.

As he sees the punt slide away into the night Stitheard feels despair so utter that he tries to cry out to them to stop, to let him go with them, but the air is as empty as before. He tries to throw himself into the water but suddenly Franco and Hunred have him by the arm and haul him upright, pulling him back up the bank and through the trees.

'Come, Stitheard! We have not lost them! Remember! Remember what we planned!

Franco keeps up a stream of encouragement in his ears, till something responds in him and he stumbles upright. The physician's steadying arm is still about him as they clamber through the wood till at last they are clear of it. They pause a moment to gather – Edmund is beside them, then the Abbot and Hunred. They cast about in the darkness to find their way down to the river. They can hear noises from the town and see occasional flames leaping into the black sky, lighting clouds of pale smoke billowing upwards. They strain to hear the sound of the river water. They pick up a track that leads to the Wall, and the bridge that carries it over the river. Just beyond, they find the wide gravel bank where Leofric and Ceolfrith have hauled the punt ashore and stand, together with Felgild, pale-faced in the darkness, waiting.

They carry the coffin through the night, driven by a terror stronger than exhaustion. For half the night they are on the straight road laid by the Romans, cutting through the flat vale of the Eden. Then the Abbot leads them onto a track into the open countryside, till they are far from the road. Soon after dawn, they reach a settlement of a few huts by a stream. At first, they think the villagers are sleeping still, but they find the doors hanging open and the huts deserted. Inside, they find food half prepared and hearth fires still smouldering. The Abbot steps forward, staggering with fatigue.

'They have fled the Danes', he says. 'We can stay here.'

They lay down the coffin. At once the last of their strength is gone and they drop down anywhere – a corner, a rough straw bed – anywhere they can fall at last to sleep.

Stitheard sinks at once into a profound and silent sleep, till he finds himself deep in the waters of a great river, borne along on a dark current that is taking him far away. As he is carried along, he finds himself being pushed aside by the prow of a ship as it glides past, so that he sinks down for a moment into the water. When he struggles up to the surface again, he sees the ship is full of strange, still people, with white faces and grey tattered clothes. Their hands are bound like slaves so that they cannot move or stir, and they gaze past him blank and unseeing. Their grave, sad faces fill him with unbearable sorrow as he watches the ship move silently forward on the current, carrying them onwards till they are consumed by the darkness, and he finds himself washed ashore, with the water lapping at his feet and tears running down his face.

When he wakes, it is dark again, as if the night has been endless. Hunred and Leofric are moving about already, bringing up the hearth fire and cooking something in a pot. The sounds seem far away in his silent world. He sees Edmund, still asleep, his face filthy. Then he hears Felgild coughing. In between the coughs his breath comes in little panting gasps. The sound causes a pang in him and he pulls himself up, groaning with the pain of his injuries. In the corner of the hut he can make out Franco sitting by the sick man, trying to help him drink. Poor Felgild, he thinks, and then the recollection of what has happened floods in upon him. He tries calling out to Franco, but the sound stays locked tight in his throbbing head. He stares helplessly, speechless, soundless. He is adrift in silence.

11

by Derwent Water

Crossthwaite in Cumbria, may 877

There was a holy priest called Hereberht, long bound to Cuthbert in spiritual friendship, living the hermit's life on an island in that great lake from which the River Derwent flows. He used to come to Cuthbert every year to take counsel about his eternal salvation. Hearing that he was staying at Carlisle, Hereberht came to him, seeking as usual to be fired with an ever-increasing love for the things of Heaven.

Bede's 'Life of Cuthbert', Chap. 28

ABBOT EADRED STEPS OUT OF THE LITTLE CHURCH after Prime and pulls his cloak more tightly round him. It is not yet dawn, though he can just make out the outline of the mountains looming behind the village. A light rain is falling as the brothers slip away quickly to their huts. Eadred is lodged with the elder of the village, in his hall – hardly a hall, but with room enough to curtain off a private space for the Abbot. He lags behind the brothers, still stiff from kneeling. When they first arrived at Crossthwaite, he could hardly walk for the pain in his hips and legs. Perhaps, he had thought then, this is my penance. Certainly, it had distracted him from the anguish of his thoughts. Now, it was no more than a stiffness, a rheumatic twinge on a damp morning.

Back in the hall, the women are making up the fire. The room is cold and there is a bitter smell of stale smoke. He bids the women 'Good morning!' and moves behind the curtain to his chamber. They have put up a table and bench for him, so that he has space to study. But for now, he sits on the bed and chafes his calves to ease the

59

stiffness, as Beornric used to do. How he misses Beornric! Always there, always ready with a fur to warm him, or a hot posset. There is no telling where he was when the attack happened. He might have managed to flee, or he might have been captured and taken to the slave markets in Dublin. Please God not killed, he prays often.

It is two months by his reckoning since they fled Carlisle. In the desperation of the first days of their flight, while they hid in the deserted hamlet and the brothers waited for Felgild to breathe his last, he had conceived the idea of bringing the relics here to Crossthwaite. He knew the church still had lands here, close to Derwent Water. In the early days a holy priest, Hereberht, had come from Carlisle to live a hermit's life, and he chose to make his cell on a wooded island in the lake. Saint Cuthbert loved him as a brother and had given lands for his support. Surely, Eadred had thought, the Saint's protection would be over Hereberht's land.

It seems astonishing to him now that he had managed to form any plan at all – when he had felt his heart so close to breaking, when he had just suffered the destruction of his life's work, of all his hopes and dreams. He had betrayed his bishop and the brothers by his blindness and arrogance. Yet, with God's help, he has led them to safety. It is a consolation of a sort. The little village by the lake has proved a safe refuge. Great mountains rise up on every side to protect them from the Danes. There is a church already, built for another saintly fugitive of long ago, Saint Mungo, and the folk are good Christians. They have taken the brothers into their homes without a murmur – overjoyed, in fact, to have the Saint's relics in their church. The brothers are working together to build a hut next to the church to act as chapterhouse and workshop while they live here. When it is finished they can start to work the land, just as the Saint himself did while on his retreat on Inner Farne. It will not be for ever.

For a while he had clung to the hope that if the church and the fort were still standing at Carlisle they could rebuild; they could fortify it more effectively and then they could return. But he had been deluding himself. The messengers told him that the people believed the town was cursed, and no one would return there. The ruins stood blackened and empty, with rooks cawing in the rafters and the rain washing the blood of the slaughtered into the ground. He shudders to think of it. If they have been driven from their home with such sacrilegious desecration, it is better never to return; better to shake the dust from their feet and find a new home where the Saint's relics can shine again in glory. A plan is forming in his mind, a plan for his own future, and the Saint's.

He feels an awkwardness in discussing the plan with Hunred. The business of Aedwulf's letter, asking that the Saint's relics be moved from Carlisle, hangs unspoken between them. Eadred cannot fault Hunred's action, in laying plans for their escape, but now he finds it hard to trust his obedience. Hunred has started to adopt some of Aedwulf's ways. He listens attentively, nods, understands what is proposed – but he makes no response, expresses no opinion, or vouchsafes some pious 'If God wills'. Eadred finds it impossible to know what he thinks. He feels closer to Edmund – a man of his own age, who thinks as he does. He is a frequent visitor to Eadred's little chamber and Eadred knows he will soon be here to share his woes. The work on the chapter house building is a daily torment to him.

As soon as the work period is over, Eadred sees Edmund's hand push back the curtain. As he enters, Eadred feels a small shock at his appearance. The brothers have always been tonsured and beardless and Eadred is accustomed to seeing all the brothers smooth shaven. But a tonsured head makes a monk immediately conspicuous to the Danes, so the brothers, and the Abbot himself, are no longer shaving their heads or cheeks. Edmund's half-grown beard and wavy grey hair give him a wild look that Eadred finds hard to get used to. His eyebrows have become bushy, half overhanging his small eyes. Like a wild boar, thinks Eadred and immediately banishes the thought.

He gestures him to the stool by the table. Edmund sits heavily and thrusts his long hands across the table at the Abbot.

'Look, Abbot – look at them! I will never write again. I have got churl's hands now. They are like leather. How can I move a quill?'

There are tears in his eyes. Writing is his only love, his only passion – the gossamer trace of colour on parchment, the voluptuous radiance

61

of ochre and indigo, the straight noble letters in procession across the page. How strange, thinks Eadred, that work so delicate and beautiful should come from these big, clumsy hands.

Eadred soothes him. 'Don't worry – don't worry, my dear brother. The skin will soften, you will be surprised. You have no rheumatism, do you? It is only the skin. You will soon be writing again, brother – you and Leofric. There are men who would give much for your skills.'

Edmund stares at him sceptically, unconsoled. Eadred decides to try his views.

'We have suffered a mortal blow, Edmund, and we suffer still. But with God's help we will find a true home for the Saint – where the relics will receive honour, and where pilgrims can come and go in safety.'

He pauses. Edmund is curious. Eadred leans confidentially across the table.

'I have been blind, my dear brother – blind. I have believed that the only place for the Saint was here, in Northumbria. But why should that be? The relics of Saints are carried far and wide, to every Christian land. Northumbria is at the mercy of the heathen, and Earl Ricsige has turned his back on the church. Let us look instead to the Kingdom of Wessex, to King Alfred. He is the only King of all the Saxons to defend his kingdom from the Danes. He is a man of learning and piety, who honours the church and sets great store by holy relics.'

Eadred has taken him by surprise and Edmund is astounded. 'To Wessex? King Alfred? But, Abbot, surely, the West Saxons have scarcely heard of Cuthbert!'

'The ordinary folk may be ignorant, Edmund, but the King is known to have particular devotion for the Saints and will certainly be eager for the relics. He is a scholar, he owns a library, and he has written commentaries in his own hand, but hardly has the scribes to copy them. You would be assured of honour and position, Edmund.'

Edmund rubs his calloused fingers together in confusion. Suddenly an entirely different idea seizes him, and now it is his turn to surprise Eadred. He bursts out in excitement, 'My lord – if we are to leave Northumbria – why, Abbot, would not our true home be across the seas in Ireland? It is the very heart of our tradition, and so many great monasteries! Could we not go to Durrow? Their scriptorium is famous! I myself have taught one of their scribes– he came to Lindisfarne to study with us, a most gifted man. Bishop Aedwulf knew his Abbot, knew him well. They would welcome us with open arms.'

'But the Danes, my dear Edmund! Dublin is their greatest port! It is infested with the Danes, the Norse – every sort of Viking adventurer. How could we find safety there?'

'As safe there as Wessex, Father. The Danes mean to take Wessex – take the kingdom, not just a port. Durrow is inland, Abbot. The King of Connaught is strong – he has driven the heathen out of his kingdom altogether.'

This is unexpected. Eadred meant to enlist Edmund's support, not have him fly off on some other hare-brained idea. It is his own fault, he sees at once. He is isolated here and it is tempting to discuss his thoughts with the brethren. But this is what invariably happens. Everyone wants to air their opinions and ideas. He realises he should have kept this to himself till he could present the arrangements to them.

'Indeed, indeed, brother, although I have a notion that Connaught is some way west of Durrow. Still, it is a most interesting idea – most interesting. I must not keep you now, but I will consider it very carefully.'

Edmund sees that the discussion is closed and reluctantly withdraws. Eadred feels a sudden pang of longing to talk to Aedwulf, to feel his bright, penetrating attention and his ready understanding. He will not oppose me, Eadred knows suddenly. In spite of Carlisle. Rising, he goes to his chest and draws out quill and parchment. The port at Derwentmouth is only a two-day journey away, and from there a messenger may take ship to Wessex and be at Alfred's court within a week. He settles himself at the table and starts to write.

Outside, in their workshop next to the church, Stitheard works the adze rhythmically to and fro, smoothing down the split wood of a beam ready to set it in place. It is pine wood and a sweet balsamic odour rises from the shavings curling off the blade. It is raining lightly, a fine mist of damp that settles on his hair and the stubble of his new beard. Ceolfrith is beside him, stripping the bark off the next long beam. He is whistling softly to himself, more absorbed in his tune than the work. At last he loses concentration altogether, straightens up and launches into a song. Stitheard continues work for a few more moments, and then joins in, his voice clear and strong. Their singing rings out clearly across the valley and one of the girls fetching water from the stream turns to look back at them. When they finish their song, they glance at each other and laugh. Hunred is straddled over a cross beam showing Leofric how to lash a truss and sees the girls too. He pauses and calls down to them,

'There is no harm in a song, brothers. But remember what you are here for.'

Leofric glares at them. Ceolfrith mutters in contrition and bends back to his work. Stitheard takes up the adze again, still humming to himself. He loves to sing with Ceolfrith. The words fly out with not a pause or stutter, and Ceolfrith knows a thousand songs. It frees Stitheard from the daily struggle with words that stick stubbornly in his throat and will not budge, or else they come clattering out all together so that no one can make sense of them. But he can sing. Ceolfrith had been certain of that. Every day, he had sung to him – psalms, songs, scops* – coaxing and teasing him to join in, till at last he gave in. What a shock of joy it was to hear his voice!

Edmund glowers at them in annoyance as he returns to work, still agitated from his conference with the Abbot. He would like to shout at them to stop their noise altogether. But at the moment he is struggling with the long branches he has to get into position and will need to ask for help soon. The upright beams for the frame of the building are in place now, so he is working on the daub and wattle

* Anglo-Saxon epic verse and ballads.

walls. It is a light job, driving in staves and then weaving the whippy willow branches between them that have been brought up from the lakeside. But his fingers, so deft and nimble with a quill, are clumsy here. He wears a pair of leather mittens to try and protect his hands, and because of them he cannot make a tight, firm weave. Stitheard glances across at him as he works his beam, waiting for the moment to help him out. All his past animosity has gone and he pities Edmund now. He pities his age and feebleness, his misery with their new life where all his artistic skill and importance is worth nothing.

As for himself, he has no desire to be anywhere else. Although he is a man now, twenty years old, his dreams and ambitions have vanished. There is a silence within him, a darkness which sometimes threatens to draw him down altogether into its depths. At those times he goes into the low stone church where the Saint lies and props his back against the coffin. Or, at night, he sits with Ceolfrith by the hearth fire, and, absorbed in telling some tale or saga, the fire-bright face of his brother draws him back from the shadows.

He and Ceolfrith are lodged together in the village with an old couple of fifty years or more. Sharing the hut has brought him close to Ceolfrith, despite their differences. While Stitheard has a deftness that makes any task natural to him, and is at home in his body, Ceolfrith seems half absent from his, lost in dreams and fantasies. He takes little notice of his surroundings and he will often bump into a table or knock a dish over in his abstraction. When he eats, he will often forget the bread in his hand for five minutes or more while he talks or falls into a reverie; sometimes Stitheard can bear it no longer and shoves the bread into his mouth. Ceolfrith will then turn and laugh apologetically and try his best to concentrate on what he is doing.

'I'd starve without you', he teases Stitheard. 'We poets are not meant for this world!'

Their hosts love the two men, filling the hut with song and laughter. Their own children are long since married and gone, and so they treat them like sons. The old wife makes savoury stews for them and her husband nags at them to help him mend the roof or fetch the geese home. The Abbot has decreed that they should not rise for the Night Offices while they are living with the folk, and so they sleep uninterrupted through the night – a period of blissful sleep of long nights under warm furs and blankets. When Stitheard wakes, there is wood smoke in his nostrils and the warm stale hut stink of sweat and sleep. The old woman chafes her cold fingers at the fire, turning a barley cake on the hot stones. It is as if he never left his village, never left his father's hut, never made the long journey through the dark to Lindisfarne. Images of his life on the Island float through his dreams: a dark line of monks filing through the church, the wide glittering water of the Sound, or Alric's face looking up at his copy – but the ring is the only solid testimony of his dreams. The warm circle of gold next to his belly has grown so familiar that he hardly notices it. Of Carlisle, he thinks not at all: sometimes he interrogates his memory, looking for traces, but there is only blankness. All he can remember are the days after the Dane's beating, and Felgild, lying on the straw close to death, holding out his arms to make his farewell. As he took up the frail, damp body, he realised that he loved him, he could not bear to lose him and, as tears rushed down his face, words came tumbling out in hard little pellets. They made no sense, but Felgild understood their meaning and held him close.

Franco gives him foul decoctions to heal his speech but they do not seem to work. Franco never gives up and whenever he finds a new herb, Stitheard has to suffer a new dose. He is making a physic garden and seldom works with the rest of the brothers on the building. He roams the valleys collecting plants and talking to the folk. Already people are travelling here, bringing a sick child, asking for a poultice for an abscess, or herbs for the flux. They come, too, to visit the Saint and to beg for blessing and protection. Already it seems to Stitheard that the Saint might belong here.

12

CONFESSIONS

CROSSTHWAITE, JUNE 877

IN THE SUMMER AEDWULF TRAVELS TO CROSSTHWAITE, before he and Eadred board ship for Wessex to visit Alfred. He arrives without ceremony, with only two companions and a guide. The journey has been arduous and they have often travelled by night. Aedwulf is frailer and, as he dismounts, he sways momentarily and has to clutch the saddle to steady himself. But his face is full of joy as he turns to greet them all.

'Ceolfrith! Leofric! Eadred, my dear brother!'

He embraces each of them in turn. Stitheard holds Aedwulf's slight, bony form, now shorter than him. He is filled with emotion. He is my true father, he thinks to himself. When he steps back he sees that, like the rest of them, Aedwulf is no longer tonsured and his hair is greying. He wears a simple woollen tunic like a churl.

First he must go to the church to give thanks for the preservation of the relics. Then they take him to their new chapter house, the fresh plaster scarcely dry on the walls, to talk together. He tells them the news of their Lindisfarne brethren, all separated now to kinsfolk and friends. The Danes have not been seen for some months in the north, since the fort at Bamburgh held off attack, and Norham so far is unharmed. Although there is still a Danish settlement at Tynemouth, the Danes have not settled elsewhere in Bernicia. There are tales of skirmishes between Earl Ricsige and the Danes further to the south, in Deira. Stitheard asks after Alric but there is no news. Aedwulf consoles him: 'If he were dead, we would surely hear', he says.

At night, there is a feast in the Bishop's honour. Half the village folk cram into the hall where there is food enough for everyone, even in this hungry month before harvest. When the feasting is done, the elder calls for Ceolfrith and Stitheard.

'These two are better at singing than working, my lord Bishop – we had best hear them!'

Stitheard feels his throat closing with panic, for he has not sung before a crowd like this. But Ceolfrith has no reserve and starts his first scop – an old tale of adventure. Half the hall can sing it along with him, while Stitheard can stammer out his first notes unheard. Once he is fluent, Ceolfrith smiles to him and they sing their own song in praise of the Saint. Aedwulf is delighted, though he sees the wide eyes of the serving maids in the shadows, and Leofric's jealous stare. After a couple more songs, Ceolfrith sings alone, his fine clear voice as high as a girl's. He sings a lament for Carlisle which no one has heard before, and in minutes the mood in the hall sinks into melancholy. Without warning Abbot Eadred, who hates to betray his feelings, especially before his Bishop and the whole company of the hall, puts his head into his hands and weeps like a child.

While the Bishop is there with them, each of the brothers must make their confession to him. When it is his time, Stitheard takes water from the jug in the hut where he stays. He pours it over his head and down his throat, gargling and humming. But when he enters the church and sees Aedwulf sitting below a window, with candles burning before the statue of the Virgin, he once again feels his throat tighten. He kneels before the Bishop and kisses his ring.

'Well, my son', invites Aedwulf.

Nothing. Silence. Stitheard opens his mouth and pushes the words with all his might, but nothing will come. He tries a cough to loosen his throat. No sound.

'Come, Stitheard – there is nothing to fear. Ask the Lord to help you.'

Still nothing. Stitheard stares in desperation at the Bishop, pleading mutely with his dark, penetrating gaze. He cannot speak.

At last Aedwulf rises and motions Stitheard to follow him. He walks over to the corner of the little church where the Saint's relics lie, with candles burning at the head and the foot. One by one, he undoes the leather strappings that bind the coffin and lifts the carved wooden lid. In the dim light Stitheard sees a pale gleam of bone, and the glowing letters of the Gospels. Aedwulf draws out a length of white, almost transparent, silk cloth. Closing the coffin again, he nods to Stitheard to sit on a stool. For a moment he stands holding the cloth between his hands as he says a prayer. Then he takes it and gently winds it twice around Stitheard's neck and head. The cloth is cool and soft, with a strange smoky smell. He feels the coolness become warm from his skin till he can hardly tell that it is there. Aedwulf draws up a stool and sits facing the relics, half turned away from him. They sit together for a long time, till Stitheard feels a drowsiness come on him, a pleasant half sleep. From a long way off, he hears Aedwulf's voice.

'Speak now, Stitheard.'

His throat opens and words pour out. He tells Aedwulf all that has been stifling him. He tells him of the raid, the flight, his failed assault on the Dane.

'I hated him, Father. I hated him with all my soul, and I hate him still. I wanted to drive the sword through his black heart and make him suffer as he has made our people suffer.'

'You were prevented.'

'I cannot forgive them. I do not repent, Father. I wish I were with Alric and taking my revenge.'

Tears of rage run down his face and he wipes them hastily for fear of damaging the cloth. Aedwulf is still, reflecting. Then he speaks again.

'After the raid on Tynemouth I felt hatred as you do. The Abbess was dearer to me than any woman alive – and to think of her suffering such terror, such horror … I felt I would go mad. So I cannot reprove you, my son.'

Stitheard is still, his anger momentarily forgotten. The Bishop has never spoken so openly to him before. Aedwulf continues. 'But you must do penance. Hatred is our weakness, it is not God's will. You must beg for His mercy constantly and, if it is His will, your heart will be relieved.'

He gives Stitheard his penances, penances that will keep him at prayer for hours, and blesses him. Stitheard kisses the ring and, as he kneels before him, the Bishop gently unwinds the cloth and gives him that to kiss as well. He holds it for a moment to his face and then takes it back to the coffin. He turns back to dismiss him.

'You have served the Saint faithfully, my son. You have done what was asked of you. There is no greater honour – and, although I have given you penance, the Saint is well pleased with you and all the brethren.'

Eadred keeps King Alfred's letter, which he and Bishop Aedwulf have pored over together, in the chest in his lodgings. While the Bishop is still busy in the confessional, he indulges himself this evening by taking it out one more time. He smoothes out the parchment and reads it through, relishing every word. It is from the King himself and not copied by a scribe; the clear hand announces his character vividly to Eadred. He is decisive, cultured, intelligent – and he is eager to welcome the Saint and his monks to Wessex. He will order a monastery to be built at the isle of Athelney, the most secure place in his kingdom. He assures the Bishop and Abbot that they will be received with honour at his court and given land to support them. The firm flourish of his signature and the great maroon circle of the seal fill Eadred with satisfaction.

He and Aedwulf are to travel down to Wessex by sea, for the King is confident that the ships of his new navy have secured the seas from the Danes. They will be taken to meet the King and will then travel to Athelney to decide on the site of the new monastery. Afterwards Aedwulf will return to his duties in Northumbria, but Eadred will remain at Alfred's court and learn the ways of the kingdom. When the monastery building is ready, he will send for the brethren to travel south with the relics.

The King's generosity exceeds Eadred's wildest hopes, but then, he has heard that Wessex is so backward that the King has been forced to send to Frankia for clergy. Little wonder then, that he is ready to welcome the Northumbrian monks.

He is aware that not all the brothers share his enthusiasm. Edmund is still hankering for Ireland. Leofric supports Edmund, of course, but the others are silent. And silent about Wessex too. Given half a chance, they would drift along in Cumbria, drift away into secular life – and the Saint would fall into utter obscurity. It takes determination, he muses; a sense of purpose. He knows that Aedwulf believes in him still, in spite of Carlisle. His support for Eadred has never wavered, although Eadred knows his dark eyes see straight through to all his flaws and weaknesses. It would not have been surprising if Aedwulf had taken the brethren back into his own care, for certainly, he commands their love and loyalty to an extraordinary degree. Why does Aedwulf trust him, Eadred, so highly? A wave of gratitude towards his Bishop sweeps over him. It is almost humbling.

The light is fading in the church and Aedwulf is tiring. Tomorrow, before he and Eadred travel to Derwentmouth to board ship, he will have to rest. He gathers himself for the last confession as Leofric comes down the aisle towards him. He is a short man, round-shouldered from years of bending over documents. His stooping gait and receding hair make him look older than his thirty-five years.

His confession is punctilious and severe, a list of misdemeanours and petty weaknesses. When he has finished, Aedwulf admonishes him and gives a mild penance. Leofric kneels to kiss his ring and rises to leave, but the Bishop stays him.

'What is on your mind, Leofric?'

'Nothing, my Lord.'

'Do not hold back, Leofric. It may be some time before you see me again.'

Leofric hesitates, then blurts out, 'It is our life here, Lord Bishop –

why, we do not keep the Rule. Because we stay with the lay folk, we do not observe the night offices. Although the chapter house is finished, now we have to do field work. You would hardly know that we are in holy orders, my Lord.'

Now that he has started to talk, his agitation grows. 'There is no respect for seniority. Ceolfrith and I are of a similar age, we did the novitiate together, but he chooses to spend his time with a brother who is half his age. My Lord, I believe Stitheard is leading him astray. Ceolfrith gives no thought to his office now but fools around with a starveling churl who never had a true vocation. They talk to women, and neither the Abbot nor Brother Hunred sees fit to check them.'

Aedwulf pictures Stitheard, grown tall and straight now, with eyes so strangely light that his gaze is startling. He has a habit of dropping his eyes under his long lashes with an almost mocking modesty. No wonder Leofric is jealous. The scriptorium was toil for him, but Stitheard has an ease that makes light of any task.

'Speak to Ceolfrith, my son. I am certain that he loves you, but perhaps he feels your anger. Remember that Stitheard is scarcely more than a boy – and he needs the example of mature monks like you.'

The Bishop pauses. 'To live without the Rule is a test, a trial, Leofric, for all of you – each in different ways. It is not easy. But remember that the Saint has chosen you. As you bear him, let him bear you.'

Suddenly, he is exhausted. Leofric sees it and is overcome with remorse. He helps the Bishop to his feet and puts his arm around his waist to steady him. The Bishop lets his head rest on Leofric's, and they rest like this for a moment before they half stumble from the church.

13

WINTER IN SUMMER

CROSSTHWAITE, AUTUMN 877

BEFORE THE ABBOT LEAVES FOR WESSEX, he gives orders that
Edmund is to be relieved of work duties outdoors. Instead, he is to
paint the inside of the church, as a gift and memorial to the village.
The east wall, above the altar, will feature Christ in glory, while the
west wall is to show the heathen being cast into hell – the Danes, in
this case. The side walls will celebrate the two saints – Saint Mungo,
to whom the church is dedicated, and Saint Cuthbert himself. Saint
Mungo will be shown planting his cross here in the flat fertile valley
at the foot of the hills. Saint Cuthbert will hold the Gospels and will
be seen entertaining Hereberht the hermit. Edmund resisted the
addition of Hereberht, as he and his island home cause difficulties
with composition. But the elder was pressing, for the hermit and his
island are held in high regard locally, and Edmund capitulates.

Although the scale of this work is so different from manuscript,
Edmund's sketches are bold and clear. Leofric works with him and
both men become taken up with their new task. Although at first they
have only red ochre, woad and madder to work with the walls start
to take on a new, glowing mystery as the figures emerge from the
plaster. He and Leofric start to experiment with different plant dyes
and so the colours become more ambitious. The village folk come to
watch them and stare at the holy figures slowly taking flesh under the
brush.

The rest of the men – Hunred, Ceolfrith, Franco and Stitheard –
work outside. They have planted a hide of barley and half a hide of
oats with seed corn given by the village folk, and Franco has a physic
garden and a vegetable patch with onions, beans, parsnips, turnip and
cabbage; and comfrey, fennel, and garlic. Stitheard helps him make

a wattle fence to keep the village pigs and chickens out. They make a storage pit in readiness for their grain. Although they were late planting their crops, they have grown fast in the mild spring.

Most days, the good wife sends Stitheard or Ceolfrith down to the spring to fetch up water for the morning. The spring is beside a stream that runs out of the woodland. A bank rises up behind it, so that it cannot be seen from the village. The village girls often linger here, to wash their faces in the cool water and talk secretly. When Stitheard or Ceolfrith come, they blush and laugh and pretend to be in haste to cover their hair again. Ceolfrith is easy with women; he tells stories and sings songs for them, but shows no preference. At first the women think Stitheard is shy, or pious, for he says little as he waits his turn at the spring. He watches the soft curve of their bodies as they bend forward to fill their pitchers. Sometimes he chooses a girl he likes and catches her gaze, staring boldly as the blush spreads over her neck and cheeks, feeling desire start up in him. As the weeks go by, the women become bashful in his presence, and are conscious of his eyes upon them. He likes one girl in particular. She is young, and her breasts are small, but her eyes are bright with laughter and she has a sweet rosy mouth. When she looks up, they gaze at each other for a long moment and he comes close to her, pretending to take her pitcher but taking her hand instead. He longs to kiss her but the other girls are watching, teasing. He takes her pitcher and fills it. She stumbles as she takes it from him so that he must catch her arm and help her up the bank. He feels the warmth of her body close to his. Her name is Gudrun. When he should be at his devotions, he repeats her name instead.

Soon after midsummer the weather turns unexpectedly cold and puts an end to dalliance. A strong north wind blows day after day, and by the beginning of July there is snow on the mountaintops. No-one can remember such unseasonable weather. The girls run shivering home from the spring, and the folk stay close to their hearth fires, grumbling that summer has turned to December. When at last the wind turns westerly, it brings incessant rain. Cloud hangs over the valley and all the paths are turned to mud. Hardly a word is exchanged at the spring as the girls hurry to fill their pitchers and get home before they are soaked through. There is sickness in the village and Franco is kept busy with his remedies.

One wet day at the end of summer a messenger arrives at Crossthwaite. He has ridden up from Derwentmouth with a letter for brother Hunred. When the brothers meet for Chapter, he reads it to them.

Eadred, Abbot of Athelney, to his brethren in Christ and to his sons, the monks of Cuthbert, sends greeting and the blessing that gives life.

You have waited long for my summons, and I desire with all my heart that I might bid you to your new home without the least delay. Alas, I have ill news, for since Bishop Aedwulf departed from us to return to his see of Lindisfarne, the Kingdom of Wessex has been assailed by the heathen. A new army of the Danes lays siege daily to the towns and ports of the kingdom with great ferocity.

King Alfred bears these trials with fortitude, but he must build new defences and summon the fighting men of the kingdom, and must set aside those heavenly things which are dearest to his heart. He has told me with many sighs and tears that the building of the monastery cannot be started till he has secured peace with the Danes - but there is no task dearer to his heart. If God wills, it will be commenced in the New Year.

I know that under the care and guidance of Brother Hunred, and with the comfort of the presence of the holy Saint, that you will continue in patience and godly living at Crossthwaite. Trust in God that your patience will soon be rewarded, and that our last state may be more glorious than our first.

Your Father in Christ,

Eadred

Hunred looks round at the brethren. No one speaks. King Alfred and his troubles seem remote, like a faraway dream. Their life is here, in Crossthwaite. At last Edmund shrugs and gets up to go. Hunred nods permission and the others follow, more reluctantly, for it is still raining outside.

It has been raining for days. After a dreary August, September has brought gales and downpours, and the folk are in low spirits. The crops have been beaten down by the high winds and the ground is waterlogged.

When the rains ease at last, the brothers go to look at their fields, their boots heavy in the mud.

Franco pulls up a handful of barley. The stalks are blackened. He rubs the grain between thumb and finger, saying with a frown, 'It is soft, it won't keep.'

He hands a few heads to the others. Stitheard chews the grain and spits it out, but not quickly enough to hide the fear that springs up at the taste. It is the taste of famine. He glances at the others. Their faces are only puzzled. They have not known starvation. Yet.

'Ugh', says Ceolfrith. 'Disgusting.'

'It's blight', says Stitheard. 'It tastes like that, like mildew. It turns your stomach.'

They stare at the wasted crop. Then they try the oats. They too are soft and watery.

'We can eat the oats,' says Franco, 'but they will not keep. They will not last beyond a month.'

Hunred goes to talk to the men in the village. He learns with dread that the blight is everywhere.

By the start of November everyone is short of food. Stitheard wakes in the early hours, his belly griping with hunger. He lies on his mattress pretending to sleep, listening to the goodwife grumbling at her husband.

'How can I make gruel with this? It's not fit to eat. It's not fit even for pigs to eat. We can't live off this, God help us.'

She sees Stitheard is awake. 'It's no good lying there waiting for barley to fall from heaven into your bowl, young man. Get up now, get up and see what you can find – and get Ceolfrith moving, it's no good lying around in here. See if there's anything in the traps, go and have a look round the woods. This pot won't fill itself with a wish and a prayer. God forgive us, what have we ever done for this to happen?'

It is a relief to get away from the hut. He and Ceolfrith go deep into the woods. Ceolfrith wanders aimlessly while Stitheard checks the snares he has set and scavenges through the trees for fungus and blewits. He finds a stand of hazel with some withered nuts still on the branches. He strips them off and calls Ceolfrith over. They sit on the thick leaf cover on the ground cracking them in their teeth and chewing the shrivelled nuts inside.

Afterwards they sit for a long time without speaking, held in the lassitude of hunger. Stitheard feels his thoughts slipping away from him into a silence where he is scarcely conscious. He lets his body slide down on the ground till he feels Alric's ring pressing into his ribs. The sensation rouses him. The ring, he remembers. He pulls himself up again slowly and looks over at his companion. Ceolfrith is hunched up, motionless and pale with cold. All his songs and stories have left him; his eyes are staring and his face has grown thin.

Stitheard reaches under his tunic and feels for the ring. He lets his thumb run round the smooth circle of the gold. For five years he has carried it next to his skin, as familiar as his bones, as close as his breath. He unstraps his belt, fumbling with cold-numbed fingers, and pulls out the ring. Ceolfrith rouses and stares at Stitheard. He tries to speak but his mouth drops open in astonishment. Stitheard puts the ring in his hands. He feels the warm metal in his fingers. He stares at the dull sheen of the gold, astounded.

'Alric gave it to me.'

'Alric?' Ceolfrith finds his voice. 'How did Alric …?'

'It was when his kinsman came for him. He brought him his arm rings.'

Ceolfrith looks down at the ring, feeling the even roundness of its shape.

'I have kept it since he left. I wear it on a belt next to my skin. No one has seen it, till you, today.'

77

He takes Ceolfrith's hand. 'I will take the ring to Derwentmouth and sell it to a trader so that we can buy food.'

Ceolfrith looks at him, his face brightening with joy. He clasps Stitheard's hands and embraces him. 'God bless you, brother, God bless you. We would be dead men without you.'

It is decided that Hunred will travel with Stitheard, carrying letters for the Abbot to tell him of their plight. The elder lends them a horse and cart for their journey, and he stands beside them now, holding the horse's bridle and repeating the directions for the fourth time. The goodwife is there too, her eyes shining, clasping Stitheard in her arms for love of all the barley he will bring home. The brothers stand waiting to make their farewells and village folk come to stare or to give messages. At last they are ready, the horse shakes its head free and the cart lurches forward.

It is a two day journey down to the coast, where the river Derwent divides on either side of an island as it reaches the sea. In former times, there was a small monastery here, but no trace of it can be seen now. On the south side of the river are the huts and workshops of the port, huddled close together on the main street that leads down to a wooden jetty. The brothers catch a foul stench of tanning from a yard as they pause to look about them, and the place is full of noise and activity. A ship is tied up at the jetty where men are loading sacks and bales into the hold. The brothers have been told where to look for the shipmaster's hall, and turn the cart up a lane off the street. The hall stands on its own, with tall carved door posts and a high entrance. They secure the horse and go up to the door.

Inside, a maidservant brings them bread and ale while a man is sent to find Roderic, the shipmaster.

'There', she says. 'You'll be hungry from your journey – that's fresh-baked this morning, and there's plenty more.'

Hunred thanks her and manages to mutter a hasty grace. Then the two men reach out, tearing at the bread without restraint, stuffing it into their mouths and pausing only for a gulp of ale. They do not notice Roderic enter the hall. The shipmaster pauses at the entrance, looking at his visitors. He is a strongly built man in his forties, his face weather-tanned by salt winds. Although he is a shrewd, tough trader his hall has a reputation for generosity. As he watches the two starving men wolfing down his bread, he understands their errand without need for explanation.

Next morning when they have eaten their fill and rested, Roderic comes to see what they have brought to bargain. Stitheard unbuckles his belt and pulls out the ring. Roderic gives a little whistle and takes it to feel the weight. 'It is a fine ring – the gold is pure and it is a good weight. This will buy you enough grain to see you through till the Spring, if you are to be in Crossthwaite that long.'

He turns the ring in his hands, feeling the richness of the gold. Stitheard wants to snatch it back and to shout at him to keep his hands off. He feels as if he is betraying Alric.

'How long do you mean to stay, brother? The Abbot told me that you would be following him down to Wessex.'

'The Abbot has sent word that the Wessex King, Alfred, is hard pressed by the Danes.'

'There has been fighting this summer, for sure. King Alfred boasts of his navy, but it's no match for the Danes.'

'Does Ragnarsson command them?'

'Ragnarsson? Not Halfden. There's a piece of good news for you. The Norse and the Danes are still fighting over the port at Dublin, and Halfden was sent to hell this summer by one of his own. Ivar the Boneless is gone, and now Halfden – only one Ragnarsson left. Ubbe is the worst of the lot, mind. He slits open the bellies of his slaves as after-dinner sport and laughs at their screaming. King Ubbe he is now – King of York. They say York is a Danish town now, with hardly a Saxon left.'

Roderic turns the ring in his hands and stares at the monks. 'Ubbe has made one of his earls, Guthrum, commander of the Danish army in the south. Wessex is the last kingdom to hold out against the Danes but God knows if they can last much longer. You may have a long wait, brother.'

Master Roderic is as good as his word. The brothers return to Crossthwaite more slowly than they came, with the cart so heavily loaded that the brothers have to lend their strength to help the horse up the hills. The elder takes almost a quarter of the load into store as seed corn, for the Spring sowing next year. Some sacks are given out as gifts and the rest is shared out to their hosts, where the brothers stay. If they are careful and if they can keep it dry, it will last them through the winter.

A few weeks later before the Christmas feast, a messenger follows them up the valley. He carries a letter from the Abbot. Hunred reads it to the brothers as they sit together in their Chapter house.

Eadred, Abbot of Athelney, to his brethren in Christ and to his sons, the monks of Cuthbert, sends greeting and the blessing that gives life.

I am persuaded that you will all know my grief at the new trial that has befallen you, and I thank God that He has given you the means to relieve your suffering. I have made known to King Alfred the wretchedness of your plight, and he is fully in agreement that you should bring the precious relics to his kingdom without more delay. Some suitable lodgings will be found until the monastery is made ready, which is still the King's dearest wish.

As winter is now upon us, the King thinks it best to delay the journey till the snows are past. I will meet with you at Derwent's mouth at Candlemas, and there embark. The King will provide a ship, and I will travel to meet you, and conduct you to his gracious protection.

May God and His Son keep you and protect you with His Mercy

Your loving father in Christ, Eadred

So, thinks Stitheard, it is to be. It is a relief. Kings don't starve and nor do their thanes and clergy. The monastery at Athelney would be generously endowed with land, for sure, and the grain stores would be full. Who would have a churl's life, with starvation always lurking in the shadows, or murderous Danes falling on your huts and burning your crops? He would be sorry to leave these good folk, and sorry to bid farewell to the goodwife and her husband who love him like a son. He would miss hanging round with the girls, too, for sure; it would be stricter once they were back under the Abbot's sharp eyes. But the ring was sold now and he never wanted to feel the wolf gnawing at his belly again. Never.

14

ᚦERWENᚦMOUᚦh

february, 878

What are we to do? said they. Where are we to carry the relics of our father? Fleeing from the barbarians, we have wandered up and down the whole province. In addition to all this, a severe famine compels us to look for support wherever we can hope to find it; but the sword of the Danes, which is everywhere impending over our heads, prevents us from journeying in company with this treasure of ours. And if we abandon it, and make provision only for ourselves, what answer shall we hereafter make to the people, who will doubtless inquire what has become of their pastor and patron? We should surely die without delay at their hands, and deservedly.

Simeon's 'History', Chap. XXVII

AT THE BEGINNING OF FEBRUARY THE BROTHERS MAKE READY TO LEAVE. The weather is mild enough and the ways are clear. The afternoon before they leave, Ceolfrith and Stitheard are still busy patching the goodwife's roof where the thatch has rotted over the winter. She is torn between grief at their departure, and joy, for they will leave her two full sacks of barley. She stares at the two plump sacks, sitting so fragrantly in the shadow of the wall. Nothing could be more precious to her. They will eat barley cakes again, and they will plant in the Spring.

Stitheard stoops through the door frame, and takes up the pitcher. 'I am going to draw water', he tells her.

It is a miracle how he speaks now, she reflects. When he came, poor boy, he couldn't string a sentence together - but since the holy father's visit, he talks like anyone else with just a little stammer when he is nervous. He's quiet, though. He'll never be a chatterbox like Ceolfrith, with all his tales and stories. How she will miss him on a winter's evening, keeping her spellbound half the night! Her eyes fill again.

Stitheard walks down to the spring in the fading light. He wants to stand there one more time, alone. When he gets there he stands for a moment, looking into the clear water. He stoops down to fill the pitcher and, on an impulse, sluices water over his head and face. It is icy cold and the shock of it clears his head. He scoops up water in his hands and drinks, as if to gulp down all his longing for the place. He fills the pitcher and turns to go.

At once he sees a shadow in the trees behind the spring, a girl's shadow moving away into the woods. He quickly sets down the pitcher and leaps up the bank. He is too fast for her and in a moment he is beside her. It is Gudrun. Gasping to get his breath, he catches her arm but she does not try to escape. Her bright eyes look up at him, not laughing now but full of tears. He draws her to him, and takes her in his arms, her slight body grown famine thin. I must comfort her, he tells himself. He looks down and sees her face turned up towards him. He wipes her tears with his fingers and kisses her as gently as a child. He lets his hand slide down her back. He kisses her again, with passion now, pulling her close. He feels desire burn through his vows, but she is frightened and pushes his arms away. She turns and runs back through the trees. He starts after her, till recollection floods in upon him. He flings himself on the ground for the cold earth to subdue him.

In the morning, the brothers sing the last offices in the little church, with the two Saints gazing down benignly from the walls on either side. Once again they take up the coffin, feeling the unfamiliar weight on their shoulders and carry it out into the pale February sunshine; a year has passed since they carried it in. Outside, a crowd of folk has gathered, from the village and from miles around. They stand silently, watching as the coffin is pushed onto the cart. Following Master Roderic's advice, the brothers cover it with bundles of faggots till it is hidden, for sometimes a Norse trader will put into the port and they do not want to draw attention. Stitheard glances around at the familiar faces, now grown gaunt-thin. Some of the women are weeping; Gudrun is clinging to her mother and he cannot bear to look at her. It feels as if the brothers are abandoning them. Hunred prays for them and assures them that the Saint will bless the villagers for giving him shelter. 'Please let them make it', Stitheard begs God. 'Please send them food.' Then they are on the path and the journey to the sea begins.

Once again they are at Master Roderic's door and a servant is sent running to fetch him. He comes up from the jetty wiping his hands on a rag, stopping short to see the group on his doorstep. He stares first at them, then at the cart piled with wood. He shakes his head for a moment and then comes forward to greet them.

'Well! Good day, brothers! Welcome to you. Let's get this cart into my yard now, and then we'll take a cup of ale.'

Inside Roderic's hall, the bearers are seated at a long table and ale, bread and cheese are brought for them. When they have eaten, Roderic starts to speak. Although the doors of the hall are closed, he speaks in a low tone. 'Brother Hunred, you have brought more than wood with you?'

Hunred nods.

'Last time we spoke together, brother, I warned that you might have a long wait for your journey. But you are here.'

Hunred is uneasy at his tone.

'Abbot Eadred has bidden us come here to Derwentmouth to wait for the ship to take us down to Newquay, Master Roderic. I had believed he would have sent the same message to you.'

'He did, Father, so he did. In December. Have you heard nothing since?'

'Nothing. We did not expect to hear again – his instructions were quite clear.'

Master Roderic is silent. His expression is sombre. Something has happened, thinks Stitheard, something has gone wrong. At last Roderic speaks.

'Father, I will not send a ship to Newquay, and you'll not find a shipmaster that will. I can see that the news has not reached you, or you would not be here.'

Bewildered, Hunred shakes his head.

'Well, you had best know it. Back in the Autumn, Alfred was hard pressed by the Danes. He made a peace treaty with Guthrum and paid him gold to leave the kingdom – and so he did, and Wessex was at peace. When Christmas came along, the fyrd was disbanded so that men could go home to their families, and Alfred and his court went to Chippenham to celebrate the feast. As well as the treaty Alfred had made, it is well known that the Danes love to drink themselves stupid at Yuletide, so he had no fear of attack. They say the King had hardly two hundred men with him. On Twelfth Night, when the King sat feasting in the hall, Guthrum and the Danes fell upon them, capturing the fort and slaughtering most of them. There is no certain news that the King was killed; it may be that he escaped. But Chippenham is taken, and now the Danes hold Wessex.'

As he speaks, Stitheard feels the familiar tightening in his throat and chest till he feels he can hardly breathe. He grips hold of the table to steady the giddiness. When he recovers, Hunred is speaking.

'What of the Abbot, Master Roderic? Was he with the King? Have you news of him?'

'I have heard nothing, Father. But how could he send word? Like I said, none of us shipmasters are sailing to ports down there.'

'Master Roderic, these are dreadful tidings. I do not know what we should do. Perhaps we should leave you now.'

'No, no Father – no indeed. We will find room for you to stay here. God knows, we need the Saint's protection now.'

That night, Stitheard lies beside his brothers in the hall, watching the shadows flickering on the wall as the hearth fire burns down. They have moved the coffin into the hall, close to them, and Hunred bid them all ask the Saint for guidance. We are lost, thinks Stitheard, utterly, utterly lost. What is there for us now?

The shadows leap and dance and, in spite of his fears, he starts to drift towards sleep, sliding deeper under the warmth of the blanket. The hall is quiet, but for the sound of the brothers' heavy breathing in slumber. Suddenly he finds himself sitting up and staring at the coffin. Nothing has moved. The fire burns lower. He looks all round him, but no one stirs. He is certain that someone has spoken to him but he hears no voice. He becomes aware of a strange certainty within himself, so unexpected that he believes he must still be dreaming. The Saint does not wish to go to Ireland. To Ireland! Wasn't that an idea of Edmund's? Why should he think of that now? His mind slides away, he lies back down under his warm blanket and minutes later is drowned in sleep.

In the morning, after Master Roderic and his men have breakfasted and gone down to the harbour, the brothers sit in chapter at the table. According to custom, they sit in silence together for a time. Today the silence is heavy with tension. Although Hunred is the least inclined to speech, he must speak first.

'Brothers, we must pray first for the safe keeping of our Abbot and that the Lord has spared him from the fury of the heathen. We must give thanks that the Saint's relics have not fallen into their hands. We must give thanks too for the protection of good Master Roderic and his kin.'

The prayers are done.

'Now we must seek the Saint's guidance. We cannot return to Crossthwaite while the famine lasts, or stay here in Cumbria. Where are we to go, brothers?'

Leofric is waiting, eager to speak. 'Brother Hunred, you will remember that Edmund spoke to us and to the Abbot about the monastery of Durrow in Ireland. The Abbot was set on taking the Saint to Wessex, and would not consider it. Brothers, I believe our being brought here is a sign! We have come to the port ready to make a voyage, but that voyage is not to Wessex. Indeed, I believe the Saint never intended it to be for Wessex! He has brought us here to take him to Ireland, the home of his beloved teacher Aidan!'

As he speaks, Stitheard finds himself filled with dismay. He remembers again Edmund's enthusiasm for Ireland. He glances round to see how the others respond. Franco is shaking his head.

'Such a journey is full of dangers, Leofric. Ireland has not been spared the scourge of the heathen, you know. And what if there is famine there, too?'

Hunred nods. 'We should not undertake such a journey without the Bishop's consent and guidance.'

'It might be weeks, months even, before we hear from him. They cannot feed us here while we wait. Brother Hunred, you were appointed to lead us, should neither the Abbot nor the Bishop be with us.'

Hunred looks round. Everyone nods agreement.

'Well,' he says, 'could we not consider returning to Bernicia, perhaps to Norham?'

Edmund leans forward heavily. 'Brother, such a journey holds more perils than the ocean. The countryside is starving, and they say the famine has taken hold further north. No one knows where the Danes will raid next, so we would have to take hill tracks, and we would have to carry the coffin. We have no guide.' He pauses. 'I am not a young man, Father. God give me strength, but I could not say if I could endure it.'

There is a silence then. At last Ceolfrith speaks, his usual cheerfulness undimmed. He is half Irish by birth and he is all for voyages and adventure.

'Brothers, let us take heed of Leofric and Edmund's advice and trust that God will take us safe to Ireland! The Irish folk are renowned for their holiness and hospitality. For sure, they will take the Saint to their hearts! I believe Brother Leofric has spoken truly – we have been brought here by God himself and, though we are downcast now, He will lift us up!'

The discussion goes on, but Stitheard does not speak. He is drawn by Ceolfrith's enthusiasm and is ready to join him. But within himself, he feels the certainty of the night, that the Saint does not wish it. What can he say? How can he, the youngest of the brothers, claim to be guided by the Saint? He has no idea why he is so certain. Is it just a dream? If he speaks against the plan, Edmund and Leofric will think he is opposing them wilfully. And what else can they do? Where else can they go?

At last, when everyone has spoken their mind, Hunred turns to Stitheard.

'Come now, Stitheard – you are silent. Tell us your thoughts.'

He is silent. He does not know what to say. He stares round at his brothers, all looking at him encouragingly. They know he still finds it hard to speak when feelings are running high. At last Hunred says to him,

'Just yes or no, Stitheard – are you for Ireland or against?'

He is desperate. He stares at the floor, at the ceiling. What is he to do? He shakes his head. Hunred takes it to mean he cannot speak and smiles kindly. The discussion is over. It is decided. They will go to Ireland as soon as Master Roderic can find a ship for them.

15

voyage to Ireland

february, 878

They now began to discuss the expediency of terminating their exertions, and providing a safe refuge for the holy body, by transporting it to Ireland, the more especially as now there appeared scarce the shadow of a hope that they would be able to continue in this country ... They assembled at the mouth of the river which is called Derwent. A ship was there prepared for their transit, in which was placed the venerable body of the father ...

The winds changed, and the angry waves rose up; the sea, which till then had been calm, became tempestuous; and the vessel, now unmanageable, was tossed hither and thither by the stormy billows. They who were on board became like dead men.

Simeon's 'History', Chap. XXVI

EARLY ON THE MORNING OF THEIR DEPARTURE, Stitheard slips away from the bustle at the hall and goes down to the harbour to see the ship. She is moored alongside the wharf. Stitheard has never sailed before and he is filled with apprehension. In spite of himself, however, he feels a momentary thrill as he looks down and sees the ship. She is a long, low-slung sailing ship, her long side beams brightly painted in red, yellow and dark blue. At the front, the beams curve upwards to the tall prow, leaning forward like a bird ready for flight.

She carries a sturdy mast stepped into her centre, secured with tensioned ropes fore and aft. The sail beam is slung at right angles to the top of the mast, with the sail still reefed in. He sees that the beam is secured with several lines of rope aft, that allow the sailors to alter the sail angle, and to raise and lower it. The back of the ship is the crew end, and the steerage. At her forward end, there are four oarlocks on either side. The eight oar slaves are already sitting on the benches, leaning forward over the oars, eating bread and talking. Stitheard stares at them. How unconcerned they are. He sees that it is just another voyage for them, another long exhausting haul on the oars before their ale and supper. He half envies them. He looks to see where the brothers will go. Master Roderic has told them they will sit in the cargo section, in front of the mast. They must sit on the stanchions where the cargo normally fits, and the coffin will be strapped securely in the middle. The sailors have rigged up a low awning for it. Everything is ready for the voyage. It is all as it should be, but he feels dread in his belly.

He stares out at the sea. The day is clear and he can see the distant hump of the Isle of Man to the south. He strains his eyes to look for Ireland, but there is only the long pale expanse of sea to the horizon. He feels the cold east wind at his back and he shivers. Roderic has been waiting for an easterly. A few nights ago he sat with them to talk over the voyage.

'Aye, brother Edmund, I know you're thinking about those fine monasteries you've heard of in Connaught. But how are you going to get there, brother? Eh?'

He stared at Edmund rhetorically. Edmund shifted uneasily, without trying to respond. Satisfied, Roderic continued, 'You'd be mad to sail to Dublin, or anywhere near it. You'd have slave chains round your ankles before you could ask directions, and the Saint's relics flung in the ocean. We'll take you up to the north end of the country. We've talked to traders from there and they say it's been quiet for a long while now. Coleraine, brothers – have you heard of the Abbey at Coleraine?'

They all shook their heads.

'It's not far from the coast, and they say there are still monks there. They'll give you a welcome, for sure. They'll not let you go hungry! It's an easy voyage over there. Once you get settled, you can see about making the journey down to Connaught.'

Roderic leaned back, pleased with his plan. No one spoke. In spite of the shipmaster's easy confidence, the uncertainty of the voyage was becoming more daunting the closer it came. Even Ceolfrith's enthusiasm had waned. Edmund spoke quickly to stamp out any doubt.

'Your plan is good, Master Roderic, and may the Saint reward you. We will throw ourselves upon the mercy of our Irish brethren. Is it not so, Hunred?'

Hunred agreed, though he still looked uneasy. Stitheard had wondered again, should he speak? Should he say that the Saint does not want to go? How could he claim to know? They would think him mad.

Now the voyage is upon them and he must gather his courage. He is going to leave his homeland. He must cross the ocean and go to a country filled with unknown dangers. He must learn to speak a strange language, or at least remember his Latin. The Saints did the same, he reminds himself. They crossed over the sea to Northumbria and brought God's faith to our people. We are just travelling back again. He summons all his resolution, but the dread in his belly does not move.

When he gets back to the Hall, the brothers are making their farewells, Roderic's wife Aelfwyn is filling their pockets with barley cakes for the journey, and servants are running to and fro. Roderic has arranged for a cart and horse to carry the coffin down to the harbour, to save any labour for the brothers. The coffin is tightly secured, wrapped and re-wrapped in leather and cloth to keep it water-tight. The brothers lift it into the cart, and the carter calls 'Come up!' to the horse.

The horse is motionless. 'Come up!' shouts the carter again, impatiently. The horse does not stir. The carter curls the whip down its back, and again, and again. The horse tosses its head, but will not move. A couple of men move forward and tug at the bridle, but the horse backs away from them. The carter jumps down to look to his horse, to pick up his feet and see if something is amiss. He gives his ears a rub and pulls him forward by the bridle. The horse moves a pace or two to please his master, then stops again. The carter looks around, mystified.

'I don't know what's taken him. He's as willing as you could wish. Something's scared him somewhere'.

He stares around to find what might have scared him. Stitheard feels his own feet fixed to the ground with dread. He glances at the others. All their faces are tense. It is a bad omen, and everyone feels it.

Edmund breaks the spell. 'If your horse is a heathen, master carter, why, we will carry the coffin ourselves. Come, brothers.'

Impatiently he waves them to join him. Eager to avoid the ill omen, they hurry forward to help him. Opening the back of the cart, they slide the coffin out and onto their shoulders. The weight of the coffin bears down on them so that they can barely support it. Even Edmund's knees buckle as he staggers sideways. Roderic starts forward to help them, but Hunred shakes his head, for only the bearers may hold the coffin. They move forward unsteadily, and now the coffin seems to weigh on them in a different way. Each of them feels an unbearable oppression of spirit. No one speaks.

The walk to the harbour seems to last for ever. When they get there, the sailors lower a wooden bridge from the end of the wharf to make a walkway into the ship. They slip and stumble down the bridge, the sailors steadying them. As they come into the ship, Stitheard feels the gentle movement of the sea beneath his feet. He forces himself to keep calm, to move the coffin along with the others into its resting place in front of the mast. They lift it carefully down, and straighten themselves with relief. The sailors toss ropes to them and they lash it tightly to the stanchions. Roderic comes down into the ship to check the loading.

'Very good, brothers – nothing's going to shift that, don't you worry. And look now, what a fine morning! We couldn't have wished for better. You'll be over there by nightfall, for sure.'

He looks round the ship, then lowering his voice, 'Don't you worry about the horse giving trouble up there – he's a stubborn mule if ever I saw one. I'd have told the lad to harness up a different nag if I'd known.'

He raises his voice again. 'And these lads will take care of you.' He waves the two sailors over. 'There's not much these two don't know about the ocean. If anyone can deliver you safely to shore, these are the lads to do it!'

Roderic's confidence starts to cheer the brothers. It is a lovely morning now, fresh and bracing, with the February sunlight making the waves glitter and sparkle. It is a good ship, well rigged and provisioned, and their sailors are Roderic's hand-picked men. The coffin is securely lashed in and the sailors have covered it with the awning to protect it from any spray coming into the ship. For sure, the Saint is safe. The oppression of their spirits eases. Edmund pulls himself up to clasp Roderic's hand. He knows he could not have withstood the wavering of his brothers without him, and his thanks are heartfelt.

Roderic bids them all a last farewell and jumps back onto the shore. The wooden bridge is pulled up and the mooring rope cast away. At the front, one of the sailors calls the beat to the oarsmen, and the oars start to dip and lift rhythmically. Once they are out into the current, the sailors move aft and start to let down the sail. The wide heavy cloth is dyed with broad stripes of red alternating with plain. It drops down nearly to the foot of the mast, till the wind starts to fill it out. Then the ropes hold it aloft, and the ship springs forward as they start to run before the wind. It is a fresh easterly, and it should see them clear to the north coast of Ireland. The beams creak as the ship lifts on the waves, and the ropes rap and rattle on the mast and sail beam. By the time they are an hour into the voyage, the ship is running strongly and the brothers are starting to get accustomed to the feel of her movement. She leaps forward over the waves, the great sail filled with wind billowing above them. The prow sends spray flying into the air but in the centre of the ship they are dry. It seems miraculous to Stitheard, to be skimming through the water like this, and yet to be dry-clothed. His spirits start to lift in spite of himself. The brothers smile to each other and Ceolfrith staggers to his feet to look over the horizon. The spray from a big wave knocks him sideways and they all laugh at his startled face. When he has steadied himself back on the bench, he leans forward to speak.

'The sky is black over there! Look at that!'

They turn to look, and see that the crew are looking too. The sky behind them is growing dark as iron. As they stare, the sunlight disappears and they feel a sudden sharp wind cut through their clothes.

'The wind's gone about!' yells one of the sailors.

The sail suddenly empties and the sail beam swings sideways. The sailors start working the ropes to bring it back into the wind. The sky darkens above them and a sudden sharp sleet stings their faces. The ship is no longer moving forward but rocking on the swell. Then the wind comes howling in upon them with such force that they are knocked sideways. One of the sailors stumbles past them, shouting to the slaves to ship their oars. As the storm hits them, the sail beam bangs violently against the mast.

'Keep your heads down! Keep low!' shouts the sailor to them as he struggles aft again.

As the wind starts to whip up the sea, the ship rocks more violently to and fro. Then she is carried up on a big wave and comes crashing back down into the water with a terrifying crack of timber. Stitheard feels his belly cramp with nausea. At the back, the sailors are straining on the ropes to bring the sail down, but they are half blinded by the driving sleet. The wind catches in the sail, hurling the ship from side to side. The brothers huddle down, clinging to the stanchions to keep themselves from being blown overboard. Only the coffin, tightly secured, is steady. They can hear the sailors screaming to each other:

'Bring her down! Over here!'

'Harder, can't you? Pull! Pull!'

'It's sticking! We're never going to move it now!'

'Try here!'

Suddenly, Stitheard feels Ceolfrith moving beside him. He grabs his arm.

'Keep down!' he yells at him. But Ceolfrith pulls away and starts to pull himself upright.

'Are you mad?' screams Stitheard. 'Keep down!' Ceolfrith looks back at him. His face is shining with eagerness.

'They need help! We must get the sail down!'

Stitheard tries to drag him back but Ceolfrith is already staggering towards the back of the ship. Stitheard crawls towards the side of the ship and grabs the gunwale. He feels the wind pulling his hair in all directions. A huge mountain of water rolls towards him and waves crash into the ship. He clings on for dear life, soaked with icy water. He feels his stomach turn and a few seconds later he is violently sick. The vomit is flung away on the wind. He turns back, gasping for breath. He sees that Ceolfrith has reached the back of the ship. One of the sailors is shouting at him and gesticulating, but he starts to clamber up the mast, pulling himself up on the ropes. He is trying to reach the sail beam. Stitheard stares, aghast. He sees that Ceolfrith is possessed with a mad dream of heroism that can only bring disaster. As the ship heaves and plunges, he is forced to cling on for dear life, swinging to and fro on the mast. Suddenly, a ferocious gust of wind throws Stitheard back onto the planks. Above him, it batters the sail beam hard against the mast. With a loud explosion, it splits in two. The beam and sail crash down into the ship. Stitheard is knocked flat against the floor, with the thick cloth of the sail above him. He has no idea what has happened. He tries to move, but he is pinned tight. He hears someone groaning with pain. He prays that it is Ceolfrith and that, even if he is injured, he is safe. He wriggles sideways to breathe more easily and feels someone beside him.

'Who is it?' he shouts, but his voice is lost in the shrieking of the wind.

The ship lurches violently to the side and the nausea rises in his belly again. He retches, but little more than water now. His body is tightly held under the sail cloth, so that he is thrown up and down without respite with the movement of the ship. Sea-water rolls to and fro under the cloth, almost submerging him for minutes on end, before sluicing away to the other end of the ship and leaving him gasping for breath. His clothes are soaking wet and he is chilled to the bone. He tries to move his arm and can feel the curve of the stanchion above him. He manages to get his arm round it and to pull himself upwards, shoving the sail cloth with his other arm. The cloth gives way unexpectedly, so that he can sit half upright, with his upper body bent forward over the bench. The rushes of water no longer submerge him completely and he can breathe again freely. Too exhausted to do more, he clings on, barely conscious. Half an hour later, another lurch of the ship dislodges him and sends him sliding sideways. He reaches out again, in desperation. He finds himself up against a flat surface of wood and, feeling on it the leather of the coffin's bindings, he heaves himself close. As he drifts out of consciousness, he is at peace. If he is to find his death here, he will drown with the Saint beside him.

16

after chippenham

derwentmouth, February 878

SCARCELY A FORTNIGHT AFTER THE BROTHERS HAVE LEFT FOR IRELAND, Master Roderic is at the jetty counting off bundles of furs and some casks of wine. He glances at a man wrapped in a thick cloak being helped off the ship by a couple of men servants. Something makes him look again – and he starts as though he has seen a ghost.

'Abbot Eadred!'

'Master Roderic – good Master Roderic, God bless you!'

Eadred steps unsteadily from the ship and embraces the shipmaster. His bags and bundles are unloaded and his men carry them to the hall while Roderic gives his arm to the Abbot.

'What a voyage, Master Roderic – what a voyage! I fear I will never make a sailor.'

At last they are at the hall and warm wine is brought for the Abbot.

'No doubt you have heard the news of the King's defeat at Chippenham, Master Roderic.'

'The worst news I ever heard, Father. I did not know if I would set eyes on you again – I thank God you have been spared.'

'Indeed, indeed.'

The Abbot drinks his cup dry and Aelfwyn, the shipmaster's wife, refills it. She lingers behind him to hear the news. He sighs deeply and begins his tale.

'I was at Glastonbury, Master Roderic, at the King's command. He sent me with his clerics to the Abbey for the Christmas feast, intending to join us early in the New Year. The King is most devout, Master Roderic, a most Christian ruler.'

He pauses, shaking his head. 'We passed the feast quietly enough, until the day after Twelfth Night. We heard the noise of a troop of horsemen passing through the village, and the cry went out that the King was come. We all hastened out to greet him, for we knew nothing of the Danes' treachery. Well, Master Roderic, it was the King, sure enough, but with hardly a score of men attending on him. Their horses were sweating from hard riding and they stopped only to water them and to give us the King's orders. He commanded us to gather up what precious relics and ornaments we had and to flee at once, for the Danes would be close behind.'

'Where is the King gone?'

'He has gone to Athelney, Master Roderic – he has taken refuge in the marshes there. As for us, we made our escape without delay. I travelled with two clerics and our attendants. They took me to the port at Burnham, so that we might take ship from there. My companions planned to flee to Ireland, giving up all hope of Wessex. I had to wait for many weeks for a ship to bring me here to Derwentmouth – and it took a few coins to persuade them, I may say. Truly, Master Roderic, we are like sheep before wolves – scattered in all directions, in terror of our lives. The heathen are going to drive us out of every corner of our land. May God strike them down!'

Agitation overcomes him. Roderic lays a hand on his arm. 'Come, Father – you are worn out with your journey and your troubles. You must take rest now. We will talk again on the morrow.'

The relief of dry land and warm bedding is so great that Abbot Eadred falls into a sleep of exhaustion that carries him half-way through the next morning. But when he awakes, he is uneasy. Roderic has said nothing of the brothers. The arrangement was to meet at Derwentmouth in February, at Candlemas, and the month is almost gone. Where are they? Has Roderic lodged them elsewhere? Has he suffered all the hazards and dangers of his escape for nothing?

Perhaps, he reflects, word may have reached them of the Danes' victory. Hunred would understand that it was now impossible to take the relics to Wessex and would have ordered the brothers to remain at Crossthwaite. Of course. No doubt that is what has happened, and it is for the best. Once he is rested, he will travel up to Crossthwaite and join them there. Another summer there will not hurt, and will give him time for rest and reflection. God knows, he needs it. Alfred is – was – a good king, of course. But a demanding man, it cannot be denied. All that zeal and asceticism is exhausting. And those endless fasting days. He calls to the serving maid and bids her bring him warm milk and bread for his breakfast.

When Roderic joins him later in the day, he finds the Abbot in better spirits.

'Well now, Master Roderic – it is your turn for the news. Have the brothers remained at Crossthwaite?'

'Alas, my lord Abbot, they are gone.'

'Gone, Master Roderic? What do you mean, gone?'

'The brothers came here to meet you, knowing nothing of Alfred's defeat. I had seen two of them in the Autumn, when they came down here to buy grain. There is a famine, Abbot. It has been a hard winter in the hills and there is still worse to come, for all the seed corn is rotted. They are gone to Ireland, Abbot. We feared you dead. They could not stay here and starve. What else could they do?'

Ireland? – Edmund's idea. His heart sinks.

'I put up a ship for them, Abbot, and sent two of my best lads with them for the crossing.' He pauses, for this is the hardest part. He must tell him everything. 'I must tell you, Abbot, that my lads are not returned. Yet.'

The Abbot cannot find words. Roderic continues. 'The weather was fine and mild and we had the ship loaded before first light. They went out on the dawn tide and it was the loveliest bright day you could have wished. Then, an hour or so before midday, the sky darkened. "Hullo," I said to myself, "a squall blowing up." February is a month for squalls – they just blow up out of nowhere. But this was the worst I can remember. It came on fast – we scarcely had time to make fast where we were working before the wind came screaming in upon us, strong enough to knock you over. A few minutes later, there was such a pelting of hailstones that we were half cut to pieces as we ran for shelter. Truly, Abbot, I have never known so sudden a storm. Of course I thought of them right away, whether they would have time to get the sail down. They are good lads, right enough, and they would have the sense to let her run before the wind. It will have blown them off course, Abbot, that's for sure. They will no doubt have come ashore in some Godforsaken spot, and they will need a few repairs, I shouldn't wonder. 'Tis only a couple of weeks, Abbot. They'll be home any time now, and we'll learn where the brothers have ended up.'

When Roderic stops speaking, the Abbot is shocked beyond speech. He has heard nothing of the shipmaster's reassurances. He knows only that the relics are shipwrecked – are gone, are lost – and the brothers with them. Hell opens its darkest mouth and despair swallows him up.

In the days that follow he makes Roderic go over the story, over and over, searching in it for little sparks of light or hope. He clings to them for a while, and then despair swallows him again. Every day he wraps himself in his thick cloak and wanders up and down the shore. When the tide is high and full he longs to wade deep and deeper into the dark water until it covers him utterly.

17

Dreams and Discoveries

Derwentmouth, April 878

'COME, FATHER', SAYS AELFWYN. 'Look – this has just come off the fire.' She sups up a mouthful with her spoon. 'Mmm! It's delicious. Come now Father, just you try a little bit of this to warm your belly.'

She is squatted down in front of him with the food, so close that he can feel the warmth of her body, can smell her comfortable animal smell. He looks at the stew, steaming and fragrant. It is just the sort of food Beornric used to bring him if he was out of humour. At the thought of Beornric his eyes fill and he wants to weep like a woman. He turns his head away from the stew.

'You must eat, Father. It's no use moping. The Saint would not have wanted that. He has preserved you, for sure.'

'I am fasting, Aelfwyn. I will not eat.'

'Some posset, then, Father. I'll make you a nice jug of posset, just a drink then.'

She rises and her skirts brush his legs as she takes her leave. He runs his tongue over the ulcers in his cheek and wonders if he should drink her posset, but feels no stir in the dullness that possesses him. When Aelfwyn returns with her jug, Eadred has disappeared. She puts down the jug with a sigh.

He edges himself down the side of the cliffs that overlook one side of the harbour and settles himself into a cleft that shelters him from the winds. He can sit here undisturbed, looking at the sea. He watches the white surf blowing back off the waves in the fresh Spring westerlies, and the dark currents shifting on the water. He does not watch for sails now. He has found that, if he sits for long enough, the indifference of the sea brings about a kind of calm in his mind, a light-headedness where, for a time, he does not feel the anguish. There is nothing but the movement of the water and the pale sky beyond. He wants only to dissolve his soul into the endless space of the sky, to be lost, as everything else is lost to him. How strange it is to feel within himself no will! – his will that has always driven so clearly, so strongly, in spite of all that has happened, now suddenly cut off, cut off like a ship's rope from the shore. He feels himself drifting as his body grows daily weaker.

At night, his dreams are confused and vivid and the men in the hall hear him cry out and talk. This evening he goes to his bed early, to escape Aelfwyn and her possets, and pulls the woollen blanket close around him. His sleep is fitful but towards dawn a deep sleep overtakes him. He dreams that he is swimming through the ocean, carried forward he knows not where. Ahead of him he sees brown sails and as he comes closer he sees the brethren. He weeps for joy to see them but they gaze past him unseeing. The sea grows rough and they are flung around the ship with the heaving of the waves. Suddenly there is a great crack and the Saint's coffin springs out of its holding and slips down into the sea. The brothers throw themselves after it, clinging to it as it starts to sink down through the waves. Eadred dives down to follow them.

Under the surface, the sea becomes calm and quiet and the coffin sinks fast through the translucent blue water. The waters grow darker for a time as they plunge deeper and deeper. Then a new light starts to reach them from below. Sea creatures with strange faces swim close to them playfully, following the coffin. At last it is as light as day, and Eadred sees that there are islands below them, glowing with colour and brightness. There are green fields and trees covered with apples. In a flash, Eadred understands. They have reached the Isles of the Blessed!

The brothers set down the coffin on the grass and it springs open. The Saint steps out, uncorrupted, and smiles at Eadred.

He sleeps late, and does not hear the shouting and commotion of men approaching the hall till the doors burst open and Roderic's bellowing rings through the rafters.

'Abbot! Lord Abbot! We have news! There is news, Abbot!'

Eadred sits up in his tunic, dazed and befuddled with sleep.

Roderic cannot wait for him to compose himself. 'My lads are returned, Abbot! The brothers are safe!'

He stumbles down beside Eadred, catches him into his arms and squeezes him so tightly that Eadred's ribs creak. Men come running into the hall behind Roderic and the place is in an uproar. In minutes Aelfwyn is at Roderic, scolding and tugging at him.

'Why, poor man, he is scarcely woken and you knocking all the breath out of him! You'll kill him with the shock if you don't have a care! Let him be, now.'

Pushing Roderic away, she finds Eadred's robe and brings him warm milk to drink, till at last he is ready to sit at the table and hear the tale the sailors have brought. Half the village cram into the hall to listen and the two lads are flushed with all the attention. Roderic bids the older one speak.

'The brothers are at Whithorn', he begins, not sure where to start his tale.

'Whithorn!' exclaims Eadred, astonished. Whithorn – the first great monastery of Ninian, the most westerly monastery of the see of Northumbria, looking out to the hills of Ireland. Nothing had been heard of Whithorn for a decade or more. He had thought it long since abandoned.

'Yes, Father. The ship was washed in to a bay further down the coast from the town. When the people who took us up heard the men were monks they took them to Whithorn. The land all about was taken by the Norsemen long ago, but they let the monks be.'

'What of the brothers?' Eadred manages. 'Are all the brothers safe?'

The two sailors are silent for a moment. The younger one speaks finally. 'We lost one man, Father. It was his own fault, we could not stop him. It was the tall one, who tells tales and makes songs. When the storm blew up, we went to take in the sail. We had it half way in, when it jammed fast. The ship was rocking so wild, you could not get up the mast to free it. All of a sudden he leapt forward and started to climb. We tried to pull him back but he went at it like a madman. It was too much for him – too much for any man. He couldn't climb high enough and he ended up just hanging there, clinging on to the ropes. Then a gust struck us that took the ship right out of the water. She came slapping down and the waves fell in on us. I thought we were done for. The beam cracked in two and that brought the sail toppling down into the ship. We were half drowned under the sail and we expected every minute the ship would go down. We could not stir. We lay there till the storm dropped. When it was steady enough we pushed the sail off as best we could and let the ship drift. He was gone, Father. We reckon that the big gust knocked him clean overboard.'

Ceolfrith, thinks Eadred, the teller of tales, the singer with the silver voice, the dreamer of heroic deeds. Alas, alas for Ceolfrith. Tears rush to his eyes and the hall falls silent.

The older lad speaks again. 'Another one was injured, too. The old man, who was so set on Ireland. Part of the mast came down on him and crushed his leg. Nasty injury, it was. He bore it bravely though. At the end they put him in the cart with the Saint's coffin to take him up to Whithorn.'

Eadred feels light-headed and grips the table. He mumbles, 'The Saint – the coffin – is it unharmed?'

'Yes, Father. The coffin was held tight under the sail and came ashore as good as new. Here's another miracle – when the brothers came to open it, the Gospel book was still inside, a bit of dampness on the pages but fine and bright as ever.'

The joy that shoots up within him sends him reeling. He is giddy, but his head is full of light. He turns and sees that the Saint is standing at the back of the hall, smiling at him. He cries out and leaps up to meet him.

When he next comes to himself, he is on his bed in the hall and sunlight is bright in the doorway. He is at the gates of Paradise, he thinks, and joy floods through him again. Aelfwyn sees his eyes open and is beside him in an instant.

'God preserve him, he is alive!' she cries. 'Dear Father, we thought we had lost you! All that fasting and wandering, and then the shock of the news. Well, there's no need for fasting now, the good Lord has preserved them. Come now, take some of this broth.'

She props him up and rubs his cold hands, warming them with her breath, wrapping a fur round his shoulders. He is alive, he understands, and his heart is as light as a child's.

18

kinᴢ alfred

ecᴢbryhcesscan, may 878

Saint Cuthbert appeared to Alfred, King of the West Saxons, in a manifest vision ... his words were these:

'I especially exhort you to observe mercy and justice, since, by God's gift, the rule of the whole of Britain shall be placed at your disposal. If you are faithful to God and to me, I shall become to you an impenetrable shield, by means of which you shall be enabled to crush all the power of your enemies.'

Simeon's 'History', Chap. XXV

THE SPRING COMES EARLY TO THE SOFT LANDS OF WESSEX. Though May is only a few days old, many of the trees are already in full leaf along the wooded hillside that slopes down into the valley at Ecgbryhtesstan, some fifteen miles from Chippenham. Here, two ancient sarsen stones leaning one against the other mark the court of an earlier king, in the wide valley that forms a natural meeting place. It is here that Alfred has chosen to gather his forces for the assault on Guthrum's army. All day the men of the fyrds of Somerset, Hampshire and Wiltshire have been moving into the valley, along the old Roman road that runs across the downs to Chippenham, filing past him to swear their oaths.

Alfred is twenty-nine, and for the last seven years he has been defending his kingdom from the Danes. He is often on horseback, and stands now by the stones with his legs apart as if he were still mounted. He is a thin man, for he has an affliction in his belly that often pains him too much to eat. But he is no weakling and he does not shrink from warfare. There is a strong set to his jaw and a restlessness in his eyes as he watches the men pass before him. He fingers the pale stubble on his chin. He has been unshaven for days now, but he means to go into battle clean shaven, with his hair cut short, like a Christian. He stands there at the stones, his clerics behind him counting off the men, until the twilight closes in and it is time to withdraw to his camp.

As the shadows lengthen into darkness, he sits outside by the camp fire watching the first stars appear in the night sky. He is afraid. Although he will ride behind the shield wall and will have a guard of mounted warriors around him, once the fighting starts nothing is certain. If the shield wall breaks, every Dane will seek the glory of slaying the King. He is afraid, but fear is not new to him. It is like the torment of his bowels when his sickness is upon him; it strengthens his will. The attack on Chippenham might have broken him. Instead, it has brought about in him an intensity that burns day and night, an intensity of will directed at the defeat of the heathen. He does not doubt that God has chosen him for his task.

Now the valley is full of men, and scores of fires glow in the darkness. They are ready and he, Alfred, must lead them. He feels in them the same will as his own, the same anger burning against the Danes. There have been too many crops despoiled, homes burned and cattle stolen; too many oaths broken and hostages killed. Since the men of Devon captured the hrefn* at Cynuit and killed Ubbe Ragnarsson, the fighting will of the Wessex men has hardened. They burned the hrefn, burned the doom-laden black raven banner of the heathen, and all of them hope that Ubbe will burn eternally in the hotter fires of hell.

In spite of his determination, Alred is not yet resolved on his strategy. His scouts have brought word that Guthrum has moved his forces out of Chippenham, and is encamped on high ground at Ethandun. There is no possibility now of besieging him; they must meet him in open battle. To the west, the Danes are protected by an escarpment, too steep for armed men to scale. Alfred knows he must move the Saxon forces up onto the ridge before they reach Ethandun. He lets his mind move over the country ahead, letting himself visualise the terrain, trying to sense Guthrum's tactics. Where will the Danish

* The raven standard of the Ragnarssons, said to be imbued with magic powers.

sentries be? Should he attempt to take Battlebury Hill, to the south, or should he wait to draw the enemy closer? He calls once more for the scouts, to question them again, but he sees no clear way forward.

At last he knows he must sleep. First he sends for his clerics to say the Compline prayers. When they are done, he settles on the straw pallet that has been prepared for him, and his guards take up their watch. They see him fall asleep, and soon their heads are nodding too. Only the hooting of owls hunting in the woods breaks the stillness. Hours pass and Alfred sleeps on. Suddenly he finds himself sitting up and staring at the starlit sky. Nothing has moved. The campfire burns low. He looks all round him, but no one stirs. He is certain that someone has spoken to him but he hears no voice. He becomes aware of a strange certainty within himself, so unexpected that he believes he must still be dreaming. The Saint, Cuthbert himself, has visited him. He crosses himself and mutters a prayer before he lets himself repeat what he has heard.

When his earls come to take counsel with him, they find a new resolution in him. 'I bid you all give thanks to God', he tells them. 'The most holy Saint of God, Cuthbert himself, visited me in my dreams and made known to me that we should join battle without delay. Draw up your men and make ready.'

19

an invitation

Derwentmouth, June 878

So then, as the Saint had promised, when the army of the Angles
assembled at Ethandune, Alfred gained the victory over his enemies, and
sent royal gifts to Saint Cuthbert.

Simeon's 'History', Chap. XXV

EADRED SITS ON A BENCH OUTSIDE RODERIC'S HALL, enjoying
the sunshine. It is June already and soon he will take ship and go
to Whithorn. He is strong enough now for travelling. But for a few
more days he will enjoy the tranquillity of his recovery, feeling his
appetite return and the strange dreams and visions fading away. He
likes to sit outside, looking down to the harbour and watching the
men working, the ships coming and going. This morning a tall-sailed
trader has come in and the harbour is full of activity.

The sun is high and Eadred finds himself dozing in its warmth, so
when he hears a man say 'May I speak with you, Father?' he thinks
at first that he is dreaming. He opens his eyes to find a man with a
tonsured head stooping in front of him. He sits up and stares at the
man uncertainly.

'Yes indeed – master …?'

'I am a cleric, Father, in the service of King Alfred. My name is Oswin.'

'Ah – indeed, indeed, brother Oswin – I recall you very well.'
Eadred peers at him in bewilderment. 'But, my dear fellow – you
are here in Derwentmouth! Have you taken flight from the Danes?
Is the King with you?'

Oswin hesitates. He has a sallow face that shows little expression.
'Clearly, Father, the news has not reached you that King Alfred has
triumphed over his enemies. It is the heathen who have been put

to flight. Ubbe Ragnarsson is dead, and the King has won a great battle against the Danes at Ethandun. Guthrum has surrendered. King Alfred had him and all his earls baptised and made him take a Christian name. Aethelstan he is now.'

Eadred stares at him, astounded.

'Ubbe Ragnarsson dead? Guthrum baptised?', he repeats, unable to take in what he has heard.

Oswin smirks at his confusion. 'It is true, Father.'

Eadred manages to regain his composure, though his head is buzzing with astonishment.

'My dear brother, we should not doubt God's power to scatter the heathen as He wills. These are indeed great tidings, and I give thanks for them. But brother, what has brought you at such a time to Derwentmouth?'

'I have been sent here by the King himself, Father. I have orders from him to speak with you and the brethren. Are they still at Crossthwaite or are they with you here?'

'They are gone to the abbey of Whithorn, in the northwest. The Saint willed it so, and I shall soon travel to join them.'

The pale cleric looks aghast. 'But – Father – why have they gone there? Have they taken the Saint's relics?'

'Have no fear, brother, they are safe and sound, by God's grace.'

'The King wishes to bring the Saint's relics to Wessex as soon as may be, Father.'

He glances round, and comes closer to Eadred, to hiss his message directly into the Abbot's ear. Eadred controls himself from recoiling at his sour breath.

'Before the battle of Ethandun, where the Danes where defeated, Saint Cuthbert visited King Alfred in a dream. He bade him go forward into battle, and told the King that he, Saint Cuthbert, would protect him. The King woke from the dream with great certainty and gave orders for the assault. He believes that the victory was due directly to the Saint's protection.'

He stares at Eadred for a moment, waiting for his reaction. Eadred mutters a pious prayer to satisfy him but his face shows nothing.

Oswin continues: 'The King believes he was at fault to delay the invitation to your people. He plans now to build a great shrine to the Saint. He will be disappointed to hear that they have travelled north again.'

What is he to say, wonders Eadred. He thought he had lost the habit of calculation but his mind is scheming already. He has an inappropriate impulse to laugh. He masters the impulse and soberly relates to his visitor all that has befallen the relics and their guardians.

'I am deeply honoured by the King's invitation,' he concludes, 'but we have learned it is not wise to act from our own understanding of the Saint's wishes. I beg the King to give me time to consult with Bishop Aedwulf and to know his will in the matter.'

He wants to give himself time. A year ago, he would have jumped at this summons and hastened to Alfred's court. Now, something in him revolts at being subject to Alfred and his spiritual ambitions.

The pale man has turned pink with irritation. 'Is this necessary, Father? Surely, as Abbot, you may decide. The King does not wish any delay.'

'Indeed, indeed, brother Oswin. The King's wish is most understandable. Perhaps I am at fault in not responding at once. But the news is so sudden, so unexpected, and my faculties are still weak from my illness. Let me reflect further upon the King's most gracious request. May we speak together tomorrow, when we are both rested?'

Oswin cannot but agree and jumps up from the bench in a little fluster of annoyance. Eadred puts out a hand to stay him, for a question is growing in him.

'Who have the Danes chosen to be King of York, after Ubbe?'

Oswin glares at him. 'Ubbe had named his heir, a young kinsman of his mother's. But he was taken prisoner years ago in a raid in the north. Most likely he was taken as a slave. So they must search for him now. Though Ubbe is dead, they fear his sorcery will fall on a king not of his choosing.'

Eadred nods and releases him, leaning back on the bench. He watches Oswin scuttling down the slope towards the harbour. What extraordinary tidings! Excitement starts to bubble up inside him. He

111

has accepted, and with thankfulness, that he will pass the rest of his days at Whithorn. But now, suddenly, everything is changing. He rises to go inside, but sees that the hall is in an uproar with the news. Roderic's serving men are running to and fro with ale, and there is a crowd of folk gathered round the Wessex men. He withdraws unnoticed, and retreats to his bench in the sunshine. He needs to think.

The Ragnarssons all dead! And Ubbe, the most brutal and barbarous of them all. 'Those that live by the sword shall die by the sword', he quotes to himself and praises God for His justice. He remembers those long ago days when he sat at table with Halfden believing that he, Eadred, could influence him. What a deluded, conceited fool he was!

Now, as he reflects on Ubbe's death and the search for his successor as King of York, a memory is stirring in him, an idea so audacious that he can hardly let himself think it yet. He sits for a long time and stares out to sea, bringing the memory into sharper and sharper focus.

Next morning he is full of smiles for brother Oswin.

'Dear brother, sleep has brought its blessings and a calmer mind. I will travel north at once to the abbey at Whithorn and give the brothers the happy news of the King's victory and his most gracious invitation to our people.'

Oswin bows, unsmiling.

'Please convey my blessings to the King, and our rejoicing at his deliverance, may God be pleased with him. Perhaps I should write a letter for you to carry?'

'Do not trouble yourself, Father. I will convey the message to the King.'

He is in a hurry to be gone, Eadred sees. No doubt he fears he will miss out on an appointment in Alfred's new Christian kingdom, or fears the King's displeasure that the relics are not waiting for him. We'll see, thinks Eadred. We'll see.

A few days after Oswin's departure, Eadred sits down at table with Roderic and Aelfwyn.

'My dear friends', he begins. 'My dear, dear friends to whom I owe so much … .'

'Ha!' says Roderic. 'What's this now, father? Are you going to leave us?'

Aelfwyn clutches his sleeve. 'Now, father, don't you think of going yet. You need time to get your strength back.'

'Master Roderic, Mistress Aelfwyn – you have heard of King Alfred's dream of the Saint, before the battle?'

'Aye, right enough – that miserable streak of a cleric told us Alfred's fine plans. You are never going chasing down to Wessex again, Father?'

'No, Roderic, not now, though God knows best what the future holds. No. Dear friends, I too have had a dream.' He pauses for effect.

'The Saint appeared to me last night and revealed to me a secret.'

Both man and wife lean forward, staring.

'The Saint has told me it is his wish that a young Danish slave named Guthred, kinsman of the Ragnarssons, be made King of York, and that this Guthred, will bring about reconciliation between the Danes and the Saxons. He has told me also where the Dane is to be found.'

He turns to his host. 'Master Roderic, I need horse and companions for a journey to Bernicia. When my journey is accomplished you will be richly rewarded.'

Roderic and Aelfwyn are utterly bewildered. 'A Dane, father? The Saint wishes a Dane to be King of York?'

'Now, father – this is just another of your strange dreams and visions. It all goes to show you need more time to rest and get some proper sleep.'

Eadred smiles at Aelfwyn, at her kind anxious face.

'My dear lady, I am certain that this dream comes from the Saint himself and must be obeyed. Do not think I would want to leave you for any other reason. How kind and good you have been to me! I owe my life to you. May God and the Saint reward you! I must leave, but I will never forget you both.'

He clasps their hands in his. 'You must believe me, mistress. I was never more certain of anything. This is the Saint's way to bring peace to his kingdom.'

20

aase

whithorn, june 878

STITHEARD PUSHES HIS PLATTER AWAY AND STARES DOWN THE
TABLE. At the far end, a monk is standing at the lectern reading
scripture to the brothers while they eat. The monks' heads are bowed
as they chew their way through the coarse barley bread. He grasps
the bench tightly with both hands, in case he should jump up and tip
the table over with a clatter of bowls and drinking vessels. They have
been at Whithorn now some five months and already the tedium of
monastery life is driving him mad. Of course he loves his brothers,
his fellow bearers – after all they have gone through together, how
could he not? But they, and the rest of the monks here, are old men,
grey-haired old men. Since the Danes came, there are no young men
in monasteries anymore. It is only the old ones who stay. No wonder
the Abbot at Whithorn was pleased to welcome them.

He watches Leofric and Edmund, side by side as usual, for
Edmund cannot walk without his help since his leg was crushed in
the storm. They are like an old married couple, he thinks. Now that
the Scriptorium has been set up for them, all the Whithorn brethren
want to sit there and learn their letters. Edmund wants him back,
for he knows Stitheard is a fine scribe and he has forgiven him their
falling out of long ago. But Stitheard is stubborn and will not use
his skills. He goes out to work in the fields so that he can leave the
monastery enclosure and feel a breath of freedom.

He misses Ceolfrith unbearably. Every air and melody reminds
him of their days at Crossthwaite – the hut they shared together,
their songs and stories. The girls. Gudrun's hair has coiled itself into
Stitheard's dreams and he wakes with the smell of her body in his

115

arms. His days at the monastery are becoming a restless torment of grief and desire. How can he spend his life here?

He knows his brothers believe that this is to be the Saint's resting place and that he has brought them to a sanctuary of his own choosing. Whithorn is a holy place already, where Saint Ninian built the first church in the land. Later, when Rheged became part of the kingdom of Northumbria, a monastery was founded here. It sits near the end of a long finger of land that reaches down towards the Isle of Man and from the monastery you can see the waves breaking on the rocky coast a few miles to the south. It is a land of grey stone and green pasture, with low trees bowed by the westerlies from the sea. Although it has suffered raids, the Norse have now turned settler and live peaceably alongside the monks.

Save for Stitheard, the brothers are at peace here. The monks of Whithorn have welcomed them wholeheartedly. Hunred has equal authority with the Abbot, and Franco has become the monastery physician again, tranquil and contented in his herb garden. Edmund and Leofric are creating a Scriptorium to rival Lindisfarne. But Stitheard can settle to nothing.

When the interminable meal is over, he slips out after Franco and follows his unhurried tread to the garden. Perhaps Franco has some herbs to help ease his spirits. But as they stand together, sniffing the sharp tang of rosemary, he cannot contain himself.

'How can I stay here, Franco? I can't pray any more. I wasn't meant for this. I am a churl and a sinner.'

Franco looks up from the herb bed and stares at his brother. He had not realised that Stitheard was unhappy here, but perhaps it is not surprising. Physican-like, he searches the young man's face for the cause of his distress.

'The Saint chose you', he reminds him.

'It's not that, it's not the Saint.'

Franco hears his impatience and remembers his own novitiate. The Rule is a hard trial for a young man, and Stitheard has no companions of his own age to lighten it. For a year or more at Crossthwaite he has lived more like a layman than a monk. No wonder he is restless.

'I will speak to the Abbot.'

'Not the Abbot.'

'Hunred, then.'

Stitheard nods.

Before long Franco talks privately with Hunred, who finds it difficult to understand what Franco tells him. His own obedience to the Rule is unquestioning. It does not burden him and he does not know why it might burden Stitheard. But he loves his brother and accepts what Franco proposes. He summons Stitheard to speak with him. They meet alone in the chapter house. With a sigh, Hunred begins, 'Franco has told me that you are troubled', he says. 'He and I have talked together to find a way to give you guidance. For one day a week I am going to send you away from the monastery for solitary retreat at our father Ninian's cave. You must use the retreat to look into your soul and find what God has decreed for you. You should continue the retreats till God's will is made known to you.'

After that, Stitheard rises at dawn each Monday with a light heart. He takes a pack with bread and onions and walks the four miles down to the coast. The cave is in a cliff overlooking a stony bay, with a high arching entrance and a shallow chamber for shelter behind. It is said that Saint Ninian would stay here in retreat for many days, and that his spirit gives the place special blessings.

Stitheard sits at the edge of the cave and lets the solitude soak into him. When the tide comes in, the waves hiss and rustle rhythmically on the smooth stones of the shore till, lulled by the sound, he lies down on the rocky floor and sleeps away an afternoon. Sometimes he roams along the shore and climbs up the grassy path to the cliff top, gazing out across the green water to the dark distant outline of the Irish hills. The silent days give him respite. Hunred does not ask him what he does.

It is an afternoon close to midsummer. There has been no rain for weeks and the land is heat-parched. Instead of walking back to the monastery across the fields, Stitheard seeks the shade of a stretch of woodland that seems to lead inland. The path twists and winds till he sees it is taking him back to the coast again. He stumbles out of the wood onto a stretch of shore he has not seen before. Little streamlets drain down from the wood into pockets of salt marsh between flat rocks. With a sudden alarm, he sees black creatures among the rocks. For a moment he fancies them to be sea monsters, come up out of the deep. A second later he realises they are cows, with long curving horns, peacefully cropping the short marsh grass. He stares, amazed.

Then he becomes aware that he is not alone. He glances round and sees a girl sitting on the rock, not a hide's length away. She is watching the cattle, and watching him. When she sees him looking at her, she calls out to him. He cannot understand what she is saying. She slips down off the rock and comes towards him. As she comes towards him he sees that she is a young woman, not twenty yet, with a slim waist. Her hair is not covered in the way of the Saxon women, but braided in long plaits behind her head. The plaits are loose and wisps of fair hair straggle round her smooth brown face.

'I am Aase', she says. 'What is your name?'

'Stitheard.' He nods towards the cows. 'Have the cows run off? Shall I help you drive them out of there?'

'The cows do not run off. I bring them down to eat salt grass. So they do not get sick.'

'Where do you bring them from?'

'From my master's hall. It is not so far.'

She is Norse, he realises as he listens to her strange accented Saxon. Her master is the Norse raider turned farmer who has taken all the land and built himself a fine hall. She looks at him, her hair blowing across her forehead. Her eyes are dark blue, almost to blackness in the sunlight.

'Where are you coming from?' she asks.

'From Whithorn, from the monastery.'

She is surprised. 'From the monastery? It is many hides away. Are you a monk?'

'Our ship was wrecked, further down the coast. They took us to the monastery.'

'What is wrecked?' she asks.

He explains. It is easy to talk to her, easy to speak because it is not her language, and she does not notice his hesitations. He settles his stance where he can watch the wood behind while he talks to her. He tells her about the shipwreck, how the storm blew up so suddenly and fiercely. Glancing down at her, he sees her listening with a little frown of concentration. A feeling of elation takes hold of him. It is so long since he talked to a girl and felt a girl's eyes upon him. When he pauses, she asks more questions. He becomes absorbed in his story, telling her everything that happened. He explains how the sail jammed when they tried to take it down, how Ceolfrith climbed up to try and right it, and how the ship plunged at once into a wave higher than a cliff.

'He must have been swept overboard.' She is the first person he has told about Ceolfrith's death.

'O!' she says, clasping her hands. 'How sad! How sad! He was your friend!'

'Yes', he says, tasting the salt of his grief again. 'We were like brothers.'

He pauses for several moments, Ceolfrith's image strong in his mind. When his attention returns to Aase, he feels a small shock in himself. Why is he telling this girl about his friend? She is Norse, no different from the Danes. She is a heathen. What has possessed him? He falters, and feels the words leave him. His throat closes. He looks away from her, out to the green deeps of the sea, the deeps where Ceolfrith lies.

Aase sees she has lost him. His strong straight body is still close to her but suddenly he is remote, withdrawn into his Saxon otherness. She feels a familiar sadness. 'You – your people – all of you hate us', she says.

119

He looks back at her, startled. She sees my thoughts, he thinks. He finds himself gazing into her face and into her dark blue eyes. He looks at her directly for the first time. She is beautiful, he realises. He sees the high arch of her cheekbones and the lovely softness of her skin. He sees that her mouth droops a little, with sadness. He struggles to find his treacherous voice again.

'I don't hate you. I don't hate you, Aase.'

Aase. He has said her name. They are both silent. He reaches out and finds her hand. She does not stop him, and he feels the small warm hand in his. He draws her closer to him. They stand together without speaking and stare out at the sea. Terns are screeching and swooping over the bay, diving for fish in a sudden arrow-swift plunge of white. He tries his voice again.

'I come here every week, on this day. I can meet you here. I'll help you with the cows.'

She looks at him, uncertain. At last she smiles. She likes me, he knows. A renegade joy rushes through every vein of his body. But then she takes her hand from his and turns away. 'I take the cows home now.'

She moves away from him, back to the cattle, calling them, strange Norse cries like the shrieking of gulls. The cows pause from their chewing and half turn round. Slowly, obediently they start to lumber out of the marsh and move back up the shore. Stitheard watches as she moves the cows along, with their long lazy strides and swinging udders. She moves familiarly among them, with a slap or a caress, pushing them on their way. She is at ease again now, her back upright, her hair bright against their black coats. Before she follows them into the wood, she turns back and smiles to him again.

21

kissing penance

whithorn, august 878

WHEN HE GETS BACK TO THE MONASTERY IN THE EVENING and stands beside his brothers for Compline, Stitheard feels his joy turning to revulsion at himself. How could he have spoken with a heathen woman like that – and worse, let himself desire her? How could he have stained the memory of Ceolfrith and Felgild by talking to her? The familiar words of the psalm accuse him and he can hardly speak. The next day he asks for confession. He tells Hunred that evil thoughts have possessed his mind and begs him for penance. The tedious rounds of prayers prescribed feel too mild for him. He wants to stand like the Saint up to his neck in the sea for hour upon freezing hour till all the feeling is squeezed out of him. He must never, never go near that shore again.

By Sunday eve, before his next day of solitude, he is clear in his resolution. But as he lies down to sleep, a new thought visits him. He has told Aase he will meet her, he reminds himself. She will be expecting him. Is it not unkind to betray her? Perhaps she will think he is prevented, and each week she will suffer, expecting him to return. Is it right to make her suffer for his sins? A new anguish takes hold of him. He pictures Aase walking the shore where they stood, waiting for him, till she believes, indeed, that he does hate her. He tosses and turns on his mattress, trying to drive the image from his mind. He cannot rest. His thoughts torment him till he can resist no longer and he makes a new resolution. He will go back. He will go back at the start of the day, so there will be no time for doubt or wavering. He will tell her that he cannot see her again, because he is not of her people and because he is sworn to God. He will bid her farewell kindly, and offer her his blessings.

When he has made the decision, he is at peace. He rolls over, pulls up his blanket and sleeps without waking till Matins.

The next morning he feels relieved and light-hearted. A calm possesses him and he is pleasant with the brethren. The morning is bright. The green countryside has never seemed so fair as he sets off down the path to the coast. He thanks God for making clear to him how he should act. He walks for an hour or more and feels no fatigue, although the day is already warm and he has eaten little. When he reaches the wood, he falters for a moment, unsure of his direction again. Although he returned this way last week, he cannot clearly remember which way he must go. He takes a path but after a mile or more it seems to lead in the wrong direction. He finds himself beside a stream that certainly he did not pass before. The weariness of his half-sleepless night starts to overtake him. He goes down to the stream, pulls off his boots and lets his feet trail in the water. Bending down, he scoops up water in his hands and drinks. Then he lies down beside the stream. The light filters down through the trees, and the running water of the stream murmurs over the stones. In a few moments he is asleep.

When he wakes he has no idea how long he has been sleeping. He starts up in alarm. Will he have missed her? Where can he find her? He feels his heart pounding in his chest. He pulls on his boots, glancing around. He decides to follow the course of the stream, for surely it must come out to the sea sooner or later. He stumbles through the undergrowth till at last he sees the trees thinning ahead of him. It is lighter ahead and he can hear the distant roar of the waves. He is still running as he comes out of the wood and onto the shore. He feels the sand under his boots and slows to a walk, looking up and down the beach. Nothing. There is nobody there. He stands quite still till his breathing quietens and he can listen. There is no sound but the waves hissing on the shore and a gull calling over the sea. He sees the black cows on the salt marsh, but there is no one sitting on the rock.

Then he hears footsteps running towards him. He turns round. It is Aase. She is wearing a violet blue gown loosely held at the shoulders with bronze pin brooches, so that her shift is visible above her breasts.

Her sleeves are rolled up and there is mud on her arms. She is out of breath and laughs between gasps,

'I see you in the wood! I see you when I bring the cows!'

She laughs again with pleasure. Stitheard stares at her face, bright with laughter, at the white teeth showing between her lips, at her half-unbound hair tangled round her ears. She looks up at him, smiling, waiting for him to speak. He summons all his strength to remember what he must say, but the words have vanished.

'Aase …', he begins, but stops in confusion.

She comes closer to him, her smiling lips upturned. All thought leaves him. He takes a step towards her and catches her slight body in his arms. His mouth meets hers. He kisses her till she pushes him away and runs mocking down the beach so that he must run after her, chase her and feel the ecstasy again of catching her and holding her. Then, suddenly recollecting himself, he holds her away so he can look at her, look at her face again and search it for evil. Can it truly be that she is a damned soul? That she is the sworn enemy of his people?

She gazes back at him, dark blue eyes as deep as the sea. Try as he may, he can find no trace of malice in her open face. He must take her mouth to his again, to see if he can taste her heathenness. He tastes nothing but joy.

At the monastery, there is no one he can confide in. He misses Ceolfrith more than ever. Ceolfrith loved women too, but had he ever sinned like this? He kept his songs and stories between him and the women he loved, so he could come close to their hearts, and yet step away. But Stitheard is in too deep to step away. He is possessed by his desire for Aase. He thinks of her constantly, through prayers and canticles, through work, through meals, and his existence is concentrated on one thing alone: his next meeting with her. He asks Hunred for penance again. The penances relieve him. He does them for her, as if each round of prayers will atone for a kiss, for an embrace.

He swears to himself he will not be her lover. Kisses and embraces are not mortal sin. He cannot help but love her – but he will love her as a friend.

He waits for her each week on the shore. Sometimes she is there before him, and sometimes he must wait half a day before he hears the cows' slow tread breaking through the undergrowth. Sometimes she will stay with him for hours, other days she is wanted at the hall and runs away after hardly an hour. He builds a shelter for them at the edge of the wood, where they can be hidden. They can watch the cattle, and see the slow movement of the tide.

One morning late in the summer they are lying there together. He has brought her hand to his mouth, and his tongue is licking the salt from her fingers, one by one. Her body softens towards him.

'Why do you come only one day?' she asks him.

'I am needed at the monastery.'

'Do you live always at the monastery?'

He must tell her. What difference is it to her? The heathen are ignorant. He takes her fingers from his mouth and turns to her.

'I am a monk, Aase.'

She snatches her hand away from him and stares at him in horror.

'No! You are not a monk!'

'I am.'

She pulls up her gown and jumps up. She starts to run from him. He is after her in a moment, seizing her to him.

'What is it?' She is crying already. He shakes her. 'What is it? It doesn't make any difference to you.'

'You are not a man.' She spits at him with contempt. 'If you are a monk, you are not a man.'

He grabs her in a rage.

'Who told you that?'

She wriggles and tugs to escape but he will not let her go. His grip is painful and tears start in her eyes. He does not relent.

'Who told you that?'

'Everybody know that. Monks lie with men, they are like women.' She is crying hard now. 'They are not men!'

Stitheard feels his whole body freeze with shock. He stares at her aghast. Seeing his face, she squirms down out of his arms, but he grabs her again and holds her fiercely.

'That is a foul heathen lie!' he yells. 'Don't you dare say such a thing to me again!'

He pushes her away from him. She stumbles backwards, loses her footing and falls onto the sand. He turns away. He will not help her. He no longer cares what happens to her, whether she goes or stays.

In the silence that stretches out between them gulls cry over the sea, and the incoming tide moves up the sand. After a while his anger ebbs and he becomes aware that she is still there. She gives little sniffs and gulps. He takes a look. She is sitting with her head bowed between her knees. He can see a red mark on her arm where he gripped her too tightly.

'Aase', he says.

She does not look up. He goes over to her and sits himself beside her on the sand. He puts his arm around her shoulders and she does not resist. They sit together without speaking for a long time. At last he tries to explain,

'What your people believe is not true, Aase. They do not understand, because they are heathen.'

'It *is* true', she says stubbornly. He feels anger rising in him again but holds it down.

'How do you know it is true? Have you stayed in a monastery? Do you think I am lying to you? Monks are servants of God, Aase. They take a vow to serve and to love God alone.'

'Why they live together, with no women?'

He sighs. How can he explain, when he spends his days dreaming of holding her in his arms?

'I am not a good monk, Aase. The others are better than me. They give up marriage and their bodily desires for Christ.'

She stares at him, baffled. He sees that the beliefs he has lived with since his childhood, and that seem obvious to him, are incomprehensible to her.

125

She turns away from him and brushes the leaves and twigs off her gown as she gets ready to go. She turns back to him,

'I do not like a monk.'

He tries to hold her, but she twists away and is gone.

After Prime, Stitheard lingers in the herb garden with Franco.

'The Norse, Franco – the heathen – what do they believe?'

'What do they believe? Can't you tell from their wickedness? They sacrifice to pagan gods and they care for nothing but battle and slaughter, and treachery and deception.'

'Do their men take wives, like Christians do?'

Franco stares at him.

'I never heard of it. They take what women they please. Lust is no sin among the heathen.'

Stitheard is silent. What if Franco is right? Maybe a Norse girl will go with any man. He cannot bear to think of it.

He is tormented by imaginings of the lewdness of the heathen. It is true that she is not bashful like the girls at Crossthwaite. When he pulls her close to him, she turns her face up to him, lips half open, waiting for his mouth to meet hers. She kisses him passionately, her tongue between his teeth. When he slips his hand down onto her breast she does not shrink away. Her eyes close with pleasure as she turns her body towards him. Maybe half a dozen other men have used her.

At last Stitheard resolves that he will do a vigil at the shrine of the Saint. He has been too full of shame to be near him, but in his torment he is desperate for help. After all, the Saint loved women too. Ceolfrith had told him that, though some brothers denied it. Ceolfrith knew all the stories of the Saint from Father Bede, who told of the Abbess Aelfled's love for the Saint. She would come to him for counsel, and would use her feminine wiles to persuade his secrets from him. When she lay sick to death, he sent her a silk cincture that cured her. Within a day of wearing it, she could stand upright, and within two days, she was perfectly well. He must have loved her.

So he does not sleep before Matins but goes to keep vigil at the shrine. A candle is still burning at the simple altar. A platform has been built at the side of the church where the coffin rests, set back from the aisle, so that pilgrims may come and stand by the shrine. Stitheard stands as close as he can so that he can place his hand on the coffin. He has not felt its weight for many months now and he feels distant from the Saint. He remembers how the coffin would lie on the hut floor with them at Crossthwaite. When he was drowning in the dark silence that possessed him, he would sit with his back to it, consoled by the closeness. People would think that disrespectful now.

He stands there for hours in vigil, muttering prayers, forcing his eyes to stay open. He implores the Saint to speak to him, just as he had in the shipmaster's hall before the voyage to Ireland. For certain, he heard the Saint speak then. Speak to me, Lord, he begs him. But the church is silent. He feels neither judgement nor solace. Outside, the birds are starting to sing in the dawn light. Speak to me, Lord, he begs. At last he feels a familiar movement of the heart, one that he has known since the start of the journey. He understands again that he is bound to the Saint with a bond that cannot be loosened. He falls to his knees and kisses the coffin. At least the Saint has not cast him off, nor will he ever.

When the next Monday comes, he wonders if he should go straight to Ninian's cave and put an end to his folly. It is a wet, drizzling day like a penance, and he is halfway there before he decides he cannot bear not to see her. He will be distant, he will not touch her, he will not stay for long. All he wants is to see her, to hear her voice and her funny broken Saxon. Then he will go, and he will leave her, put her behind him for ever.

His clothes are wet through when he reaches the sea. He finds her already in their shelter, keeping out of the rain. Neither of them speaks when he comes in beside her. She does not look at him, but he glances at her and sees her chin jutting upwards defiantly. It makes him want to laugh but he remains silent. They stand apart, listening to the rain. After a few moments she notices the rain-water dripping off his tunic and she gives a little cry, touching his chest and saying,

'You are wet!'

She pushes him away and starts to brush the water off him. He stands obediently, feeling her hands on him. A recollection stirs in him of his mother scolding him and brushing off his wet clothes in the smoky hut of his childhood. He tastes the familiar intimacy of the hearth in her brisk, brushing hands.

'There!' she says, satisfied.

And now she will sit and come close to him, and let her hand rest in his. The spat is forgotten because one of the cows has gone lame and he must help to hold her still while she puts a poultice on. He nods and agrees, hardly hearing what she is saying, conscious only of her body beside him. When she is done they sit in silence for a while listening to the rain dripping on the branches above them. He finds his voice and asks her,

'Do your people marry?'

'Yes. I must marry soon. My father looks for a Norse man for me. It is not so easy here. Perhaps he waits till a trader comes, but then he would take me far away. My father does not want to lose me!'

'How can you marry? How can I be your friend if you marry?'

'But you are a monk! Monks don't marry – or do they marry each other?'

'Don't laugh at me! Don't laugh at me, little cat!'

He claps his hand over her teasing mouth, and she fights him back till they tire and roll apart. He lies and stares at the streaks of light coming through the woven branches of the shelter. He sits up on his elbow and finds her gaze.

'I don't want you to marry some heathen trader, Aase. I want you. I want you to be mine.'

For a long moment their gaze is locked together, the light eyes and the dark. He feels as if she is his already. But she says nothing. Lifting her hand to his hair, she pulls his head towards her.

At the monastery, he passes his time in a daze, abstracted from the familiar life around him. He can sing his way through half a dozen psalms without any consciousness of what he is doing. He feels as if everyone must notice, must see the change in him. But no one remarks upon it, not even sharp-eyed Franco. As summer draws into autumn and the first leaves start to yellow on the trees, Stitheard's thoughts torment him. How will he see her when winter comes? What if her father finds a husband for her? Will she leave him without a qualm?

At last he asks Hunred for confession. They meet after Compline in the white church built by Ninian, where the stone walls keep the air cool and still even on the warmest day. Hunred is hopeful. He knows Stitheard has taken many penances, as well as his retreats. He prays that God may grant Stitheard the contentment he, Hunred, feels so abundantly in their new home. He blesses the young man and begins,

'I can see that you have carried out your retreat faithfully each week, my son. I pray that God and the Saint have blessed you with their guidance.'

There is nothing for it. He must blurt it out, get it out before it explodes inside him.

'I want to give up my vows, Hunred. I want to leave the novitiate.

Hunred stares at him, astonished.

'I'm not worthy to be a monk, brother. I know I'm not.'

'You must ask our Lord for his grace, my son. None of us are worthy before the Lord.'

Stitheard feels desperate.

'It's not that, Hunred. I want to marry.'

'To marry? How can you marry?'

Hunred is completely uncomprehending. He is so simple, so innocent. It is impossible to tell him about Aase, to admit he has betrayed his trust.

'I mean, I want to be an ordinary man and have an ordinary life, like the life I would have had if my father had not brought me to the monastery. I don't want to be a monk.'

'But the Saint has chosen you, Stitheard. He has brought you to safety here, at this house of God.'

'I won't leave the Saint. I didn't mean that.'

Hunred is bewildered. He feels as if somehow Stitheard has got lost, and he, Hunred does not know how to find him again.

'Brother Stitheard, I cannot tell what has brought these thoughts to you. You must remember that the Devil is crafty and can so deceive us that we believe his thoughts to be our own. I will give you a penance and you must use it to beg our Lord for his guidance and mercy.'

'It won't make any difference, Hunred. I've prayed and done penance all summer and nothing has changed. I know I can't keep the vows – not a monk's vows. Of course I won't leave the Saint. I'll serve him as a lay brother. It won't be any different. I beg you, brother.

He stares at Hunred in desperation. At last an idea seizes him.

'Abbot Trumwin will send messengers to Norham before the winter, so he told us. Let me go with them, Hunred. Let me see the Bishop. It was Bishop Aedwulf who took me in as a boy. He can decide.'

Hunred bows his head and sits in silence for a long time. At last he speaks.

'I will ask the Abbot. It may be for the best. My dear brother, this grieves me to the heart, and so it will the others. We have lost two of our brothers already – and now to lose you too ....'

He takes Stitheard's hands and clasps them, shaking his head with emotion. Stitheard holds his rough hands in his, but all he can think of are her hands, her small hands with their strong salty fingers.

After he has spoken to Hunred he can think of one thing only: that he must see Aase before he leaves. Soon everyone will hear of it, will be watching him, talking about him. He must go today. He can be down on the coast by afternoon, before she takes the cows up from the salt marsh.

He leaves the monastery while the brothers are singing None and his feet pick up the now familiar track. He prays to God that if He wills him to marry Aase, that He will cause her to be there. Let her be there …. Let her be there …. He repeats the words again and again like an invocation as he half runs the long miles to the shore. At last he is there, sweating and gasping for breath in the heat of the afternoon as he looks up and down the sands. A movement in the water catches his attention. It is Aase. She has waded into the sea, with only her shift on, tucked up at her waist. She bends over, splashing water over her arms and face. As the small waves come in, she stands on tiptoe to keep her shift from getting wet. Her blue gown is laid carefully on the rock.

He watches her, hardly able to believe that it is her, that God has brought her to him. He bows his head for a moment to give thanks, lest God take away what He has given. When he looks up, she is turning to come out of the water. She has not seen him. She brushes the water off her arms and legs and stands for a moment in the sunshine to dry off. He has almost reached her when she sees him. She gives a little cry of surprise, and stands half smiling, half perplexed. He catches her into his arms, kissing her, pulling her close to him. He feels the warmth of her body through the thin shift and smells her wet skin. God has delivered her to me, he thinks. He leans down and kisses her neck and shoulders and her wet arms. He turns towards the woods, but she pauses.

'My gown,' she says. 'I take my gown.'

He lifts the gown from the rock and folds it over his arm. He puts the other arm around her and half carries her up to the shelter.

Afterwards, they lie together naked in the warmth of the late afternoon, her legs still tangled round him. She has undone her braids so that her long shining hair lies round her shoulders and on her breasts. Her eyes are half closed, and her mouth is still rounded with pleasure. He leans down and kisses her again and she parts her lips with a little sigh. She has no morals, he thinks – a Saxon girl would be ashamed, would try and cover herself, would weep with remorse. Not Aase. She is like a cat that purrs when you stroke her and rubs her body against your legs for more. A little tawny cat, that can spit and stretch out her sharp claws when displeased. He laughs aloud, and she opens her eyes to look at him.

131

'Pussy cat', he says.

She slides the tip of her tongue out between her lips at him, looking for all the world like a cat who has lapped the cream, so that he must kiss her again. He feels a pang of envy for her pagan freedom, for her licentious gods who care nothing for laws and commandments.

She sits up and he knows she has remembered the cows. She peers out of the shelter to see where the sun is. Suddenly he is overwhelmed with sadness. He must leave her. He must return to his own world and the vows that bind him.

He sits up and catches her shoulder so that her face is turned towards him. He speaks urgently.

'I am going away, Aase. I will not see you for many weeks. When I come back I will not be a monk. When I come back I will marry you.'

He pauses, 'Swear that you will wait for me.'

She is still languorous and cannot take in what he is saying, but she nods to please him.

'I swear.'

He sees she has not understood him and speaks more urgently.

'Swear by your gods.'

She blinks and pushes the hair back from her face.

'Do not go, Stitheard.'

'Listen, Aase.' He takes her hands and holds them in his and speaks as clearly as he can.

'I have to make a journey. It will take many weeks. But when I come back I will be free to marry you. Swear that you will wait for me.'

She understands now. She is solemn.

'I swear by Thor that I wait for you.'

'You must wait for me. If you marry another man while I am gone, I will kill him. Do you understand?'

'I wait for you.'

He takes her in his arms and kisses her. She starts to cry.

'I don't like you to go.'

'I'll come back as soon as I can.'

'If it is winter the cows stay in the barn. I don't come to the sea.'

'Where can I find you?'

132

She considers, her face now streaked with tears.

'There is a spring under the hill, near the hall. I get water in the morning and the evening.'

He nods. Already he is shifting into the future, into the image of his return that will sustain him through the journey. He takes her gown and slides it over her head, and fixes the bronze brooches at her shoulder. There is no time to braid her hair again. She ties it back with a piece of cord. They kiss, once more, and she is gone.

22

Swords and Ploughshares

Whittingham, september 878

The blessed Cuthbert himself appeared in a vision to Abbot Eadred, that man of holy life ... and he addressed him in these words:

'... ask to be informed where you can find a lad named Guthred, the son of Hardacnut, who was sold to a widow. Having found him, and paid the widow the price of his liberty, let him be brought before the army of the Danes; and my will and pleasure is, that he be elected and appointed king at Oswiesdune, and let the bracelet be placed upon his right arm.'

Simeon's 'History', Chap. XXVII

IT IS ALREADY AUTUMN BY THE TIME THE ABBOT AND HIS COMPANIONS make their way through the Cheviot foothills to Whittingham. Guthred is ploughing barley stubble on one of the widow's fields when the elders bring Eadred to the young man. He has stripped off his tunic and sweat is running down his back and legs. He wrestles the plough share through the soil, the muscles on his arms standing out with the strain. The widow has let him grow his hair in the Danish fashion and it lies in damp curls against his face. It takes him a few minutes to notice Eadred and his companions. When he does, he slackens his grip on the plough till the ox slows to a halt, turning its head to stare at its driver. For a moment nothing moves. Then Guthred calls out to them, his English hardly accented,

'Good day, masters.'

His face is reddened from the sun. A rough pale beard hides his mouth so Eadred cannot tell his expression, but his blue eyes are wary as he scans his visitors. Eadred mutters a prayer. So much rests on this sweating youth.

'Leave the ploughing', the elder calls to him. 'The lord abbot wants to speak with you.'

As he speaks, the widow comes running from her hut, calling him in for a fresh tunic, crying to the elder to take care of the ox and plough, bowing to Eadred and gabbling blessings.

'My lord abbot, may God bless you, truly the Saint worked a miracle on him, he has never suffered again, you may see it for yourself. And you have come all this way, what an honour to us, my lord – I will send him to you … please you to wait a moment, he is dirty from the field and not fit to speak with you.'

At last Guthred is made ready and brought to the elder's hall. Eadred bids him sit as he fidgets uncomfortably on the hard bench. Surely there must be a sheepskin somewhere. He feels the youth staring at him and gathers his dignity.

'Guthred, my name is Eadred and I am Abbot to the people of Saint Cuthbert. You know of the Saint already, for you have seen the relics and he has healed your sickness.'

'Do you wish me to tell you of the healing?'

'You may tell me if you please, but I have not come to talk to you about the healing. It was the first sign you received from the Saint, but now he intends greater favour to you. He has visited me in a dream and brought me here to see you.'

Guthred is confused. His eyes are wary again.

'I must ask some questions of you, Guthred. When the elders brought news of your healing they claimed that you were of noble birth among your own people. Is this true?

'It is true, master. I was not born a slave.'

'Who are your parents?'

'My father was an earl. When I was still a child, his long ship was lost in an autumn storm, with all his men and treasure. My mother was kin to the Ragnarssons, so we went to live at their hall and I grew up there. When the Great Army left to fight in the Saxon kingdoms, Halfden took me with him.'

'Have you spoken to the people here of this?'

'What does it matter to them? I was captured, I am a slave. At first I boasted of it, I thought they might seek a ransom for me. But they fear my people, they will not go near them. They spit at me because I am a Dane.'

'They have cause to fear the Danes, Guthred. But soon you will be held in honour by Dane and Saxon alike, if God wills.'

Guthred leans across the table, his sunburned face suddenly filled with passion. He grasps Eadred's hands, his hard strong fingers half crushing them.

'Am I to be freed? Have you come here to free me?'

Eadred tugs his hands free irritably. The boy is so raw. God grant me patience.

'You will be free, but first you must understand!' he snaps. 'You must understand what I tell you!'

There is a long pause. He sees there are tears on Guthred's face and he relents. He has suffered, after all. He leans forward again, softening his tone.

'The Ragnarssons are dead, Guthred. Ubbe was the last, killed in battle against Alfred of Wessex not two months ago. Ubbe was King of York. If your people accept you as his kinsman, you will be chosen as his heir.'

Day after day they sit together till Eadred is satisfied that Guthred understands what the Saint wants from him, and how they – Eadred and he – are going to bring it about. The smith comes and strikes the slave ring off Guthred's leg. Eadred gives orders to make ready for the journey to York and early on an October morning they bid their farewells to the village folk. There is a tang of frost on the air and a drift of pale leaves on the ground. Roderic's men will travel with them, together with a guide from the village. Eadred sits stiff and uncomfortable on his horse, his bones aching already and the sour taste of the morning's porridge in his mouth. Can they not make the least gruel without burning it, he wonders. He thinks of Aelfwyn, of her warm motherly bustling, her hot possets and her savoury stews. How he would love to taste one now! He thinks fondly of the shipmaster and his generous, good-natured household. Perhaps he will return there when all this business is done, if God wills.

He looks at Guthred, riding ahead on a short-legged mare lent by the elder. He has let the reins hang loose and is breaking off pieces of bread from a loaf inside his cloak, stuffing them into his mouth. How he eats! He goes at every meal like a starving man, and then steals away bread for an after course. No wonder if the widow's food is like the rest of the village. He must have had years of these thin burnt gruels.

The widow could hardly let go of him, in spite of all the promised gold and the strong new slave that would be found for her. He was as good as a son to her, she said. He must have been kind to her, kind as with his own mother. Or did he calculate that she might set him free one day?

Eadred is still uncertain of him. He is quick-witted and has learned all that Eadred has taught him. He still serves his pagan gods, but what of that? It is enough that he holds the Saint in honour. Guthred understands how the plan Eadred has unfolded to him will serve both Dane and Saxon. But will Guthred stick to it? Is it folly to expect a Dane to keep his word? Is the treachery of the Ragnarssons in his blood? But then, Eadred reminds himself, it is in Guthred's interests too, for he is not a fool.

Whatever happens, it is a joy to be travelling to York. He will be able to rest at the Bishop's hall and recover from the endless journeying. He checks himself. If, that is, the hall is still standing, and if there is still a bishop in York.

At first Bishop Wulfhere does not recognise Eadred. His old rheumy eyes are watering in the smoke of the hearth fire and he cannot make him out with the light behind him in the door way. Eadred moves inside and takes Wulfhere by the hand.

'My dear Bishop, how I rejoice to see you here! It is Abbot Eadred.'

'Eadred? Eadred? Dear Lord, how can this be?'

He clings to Eadred's hands, staring at him short-sightedly, shaking with emotion. A serving man comes to his side, uncertain. Wulfhere turns to him. 'This – this ....'

He cannot finish. Eadred pats his shoulder comfortingly.

'Come, my dear Bishop – shall we bid your man bring us some warm ale? I have shocked you! I should have sent word to you, but there has been little time to order our coming. I did not know if I would find you here, and I give praise to God that He has preserved you amongst the heathen.'

'I did not think to see you in this life, brother. When we heard that Carlisle was destroyed, we feared all was lost.'

'The Saint has preserved his servants, I thank God.'

The ale is brought and they sit together at the table. How he has aged, thinks Eadred – but then, perhaps he thinks the same of me. He glances round the hall which is cramped and dirty. He had to find a messenger to bring him here. The town is so grown, so changed with new streets and tradesmen's huts packed in cheek by jowl, that he could not tell where he was.

The Abbot and his men had been offered lodging at the King's hall, but already the crowd in there was growing raucous. Guthred's arrival had caused a sensation. As soon as he stood in the King's hall and spoke his name in the heathen tongue, Eadred could see the change taking place. In spite of his simple clothes, his presence was unmistakeable. He was sure of himself, unafraid. The Danes crowded into the room, gawking at him, staring at his face, touching his body and muttering charms. When one of the Danish earls entered the room, they all went silent. He was a grim, hard man, but Guthred did not flinch. He announced himself again and stood his ground as the earl stared. He crossed to stand in front of him, questioning Guthred intently and looking closely at his face. At last, with a movement of his face that could have been a smile, he clapped him on the back. The room broke into a roar.

So now Eadred finds himself here with Bishop Wulfhere, his ally of old, who has started to tell his story. Eadred eases his aching thighs and settles in to listen.

'When we heard the news of the uprising, I was filled with terror, may God forgive me. I felt sure that the Danes would take revenge upon us. We fled that night – myself and five priests. Alas, Eadred, I did not even stop to secure the treasures and holy books of the church, I was so blinded with fear.

In a moment, Eadred is standing again outside the Abbey in Carlisle with the stifling stench of smoke in his nostrils. He pushes the memory away.

'We have all known what it is to feel the fury of the heathen come upon us, my dear Wulfhere. You should not reproach yourself. Thank God you escaped destruction at their hands. Where did you take refuge?'

'We fled to Mercia, to King Burghred, a most pious and holy man. He made us welcome and lodged us in the Abbey there. But I could not rest. I had left my people, left them like sheep without a shepherd, betrayed my oath. I was tormented with shame. At last I told Burghred that I must go.

'When I returned, the folk met me with so much joy! Such joy! I swore I would never abandon them again. So we have gone on, Eadred, and now the Danes leave us in peace.'

'What of Earl Ricsige? Does he still claim the kingship?'

Wulfhere stares at him.

'Indeed, Eadred, he is dead these two years gone. He and his men rode out from Bamburgh against the army of Halfden Ragnarsson, and Ricsige was slain with many of his company. Now his uncle, Earl Aelberht of Bamburgh, calls himself King of Northumbria.'

'God rest his soul.'

He remembers the Council at Hexham, Ricsige and his thanes roaring for revenge and hot for battle. It – the uprising – had all started there. He and Aedwulf should have cursed them with oaths so deep that they would not have dared to fight, and begged that the Saint strike them dead; they should have betrayed them to the Danes – anything, to have stopped them. But it was over now. He leans forward to Wulfhere,

'Dear brother, let me tell you of the plan the Saint has revealed to me, to bring us all to safety. I need your help.'

23

all that lies between tyne and wear

york, october 878

The saint once more appeared to the Abbot in a vision, and spoke thus:

'Tell the king that he must give to me, and to those who minister in my church, the whole of the district lying between the Tyne and Wear, to be held in perpetuity, that it may be the means of providing them with the necessaries of life, and secure them against want. Moreover, command the king to appoint that my church shall become a safe place of refuge for fugitives, so that anyone who flees to my body, for what cause soever, shall have protection there for thirty-seven days; and that the asylum shall not be violated upon any pretence whatever.'

Simeon's 'History', Chap. XXVII

WULFHERE TAKES THE ABBOT TO HIS PRIVATE QUARTERS. A casement window stands half open. A servant brings ale for them and sets it on the table. Eadred bids him bring lights, and he closes the window himself. He does not wish their conversation to be overheard.

Once the candles are set, the two men draw their chairs close to the table. Wulfhere mutters blessings as he looks at Eadred, still half doubting his friend is truly flesh and blood. Eadred gathers his hands round the beaker of ale and begins his story.

He tells Wulfhere of their travels: of Carlisle, of Crossthwaite and the famine; of how he and Aedwulf travelled to visit King Alfred, and Alfred's desire to make a new shrine for the Saint in Wessex; of the brothers' voyage to Ireland, the shipwreck, and of the Saint's new resting place at Whithorn.

141

'I have been slow to understand the Saint's wishes, Wulfhere – God forgive me. The relics of saints are taken all over Christendom, and I thought the Saint would be content to rest in any holy place. It is not so. Each time we were prevented. I was blind to his meaning. Cuthbert is the Saint of the North, Wulfhere. He is the spirit of our people and our protection. His shrine must be at the heart of the kingdom.

Eadred pauses. Wulfhere grasps his hand.

'May it be so, brother – by God's grace, may it be so.'

'After the shipwreck, I believed that Whithorn would be his resting place. But then the Saint made me understand otherwise. I saw that he had healed the slave Guthred so that he would become the means of the Saint's restoration. The Saint made his wishes known to me in a dream, sinner though I am.'

Wulfhere is astonished at Eadred's claim, but holds his peace.

'The Saint has healed Guthred and brought about his release from slavery. He has given his blessing on his kingship. In gratitude for the favour shown him, Guthred will give land to the Saint's people that will be a sanctuary, consecrated to the Saint alone. It is to be the land of the holy folk, the Saint's people, in the heart of the kingdom – and it is to be held in honour by Saxon and Dane alike.'

Wulfhere's mouth sags open a little. He screws his eyes up to try and see Eadred's face more clearly.

'My dear brother – why, it is a miracle! You are blessed, blessed ....' He grips Eadred's arm, unable to continue.

'I have brought Guthred to York. He is with his people now.'

'He is truly a Ragnarsson?'

Eadred nods. Wulfhere shifts uneasily on the chair.

'But ... if he is a Ragnarsson – the heathen, you know ... the Ragnarssons glory in deceit and treachery ....'

Eadred nods again. He leans across the table, lowering his tone.

'By God's grace, I have shown Guthred that the Saint's wishes will serve his interests too. Through them, he will have the means to bring peace to his Kingdom of York.' He pauses.

'The Danes have conquered Northumbria, Wulfhere. But it is York they want, York with all its trade, and the rich land of Deira that surrounds it. Not Bernicia. They have mountains enough in their own country. The Saint's lands will divide the kingdom, between the river Tyne in the north and the Wear in the South. Guthred will give land enough to the Saint and his people that will take a day's journey to cross it, in either direction. It will be a sanctuary, and no man may carry arms across it.'

Wulfhere's bewilderment deepens.

'Enough land for a day's journey, Eadred? Why, that is many thousand hides!'

'It is the Saint's price for his deliverance. Guthred must honour it. And there must be agreement. I need your help, Wulfhere. The church must support Guthred's election. We must not waver.'

24
the judgement

norham, october 878

Aedwulf walks by the river, watching the dark waters of the Tweed swirl and eddy in the cliff-side pool as it flows towards the sea. The tide does not reach the waters at Norham but today he can smell the salt in the air as the east wind blows upriver. The swallows swerve low over the water, and then suddenly swoop up together to sit along a branch, twittering and chattering as they wait to fly away. Aedwulf feels the restlessness and movement in the air.

Although the Saint is far away, Aedwulf is often aware of his presence. He has served him for a long time now. He recognises in the restlessness and movement the Saint's will, waiting to unfold itself. He feels a faint sense of excitement but he shows nothing. He waits, day by day. His physical strength is failing but his patience is very strong.

Even so, he is taken by surprise when Brother Stitheard arrives at the village with three brothers from Whithorn. Stitheard seems taller than ever, and he is careful as he embraces Aedwulf as if fearing to crush his frail body. What a joy it is to see him! Aedwulf welcomes the brothers and bids them to rest and drink after the long journey. In spite of the pleasure of their meeting, he perceives that Stitheard is troubled. He will wait till he is rested. The brothers have brought him messages and greetings from Whithorn and he takes these with him to his hut.

He unrolls the first carefully and lays it on his writing table, as he notices that it is from the Abbot of Whithorn.

Greetings from Trumwin, Abbot of Whithorn to our dear father in Christ, Aedwulf

Bishop of Lindisfarne, may our Lord favour and protect you.

We rejoice that the brethren of the blessed Saint Cuthbert have been brought by God's hand to our monastery, together with the precious relics of the Saint. Surely God has bestowed blessings upon us.

I write to commend to you our Brother Stitheard, by whose hand this comes. He has earnestly entreated Brother Hunred and myself to release him from his holy vows as a monk of the novitiate and servant of God. We have counselled him to examine his soul and conscience, and to be vigilant against the cunning of the Devil, but he is fixed in his desire. We have resolved that since he was admitted into holy orders by his own consent to your lordship, he should seek judgement directly from yourself. Therefore we have sent him with other brothers and companions eager to benefit from your authority and wisdom, to travel to your place of refuge at Norham, trusting in God to protect them and you from the assaults of the heathen.

May God and the Saint give you guidance and protection.

Your servant in Christ,

Trumwin

Aedwulf lets the parchment roll back up under his fingers, then straightens it out again and rereads it. Certainly then, the boy is troubled. He stares through the dark wall of the room, back to the hall where the starveling was brought to him, his eyes bright in his famished face. He chose his vocation then, but he was still a child, and a starving child at that. Well. We will talk.

What next, he wonders, what next? He unrolls another parchment, hoping for news of Eadred. But this is a request from the Prior at Whithorn as to whether any vestments or coverings saved from Lindisfarne might be sent to adorn the Saint's relics. No matter. He will have leisure to speak with Stitheard later and learn if there is news of the Abbot. As to the coverings, he will have his servant check if there is anything suitable.

The last parchment is delicately bound round with a covering, which takes him a few minutes to undo. For a moment he is startled – dazzled – as he unrolls it. He sees it is an exquisite copy of the psalm of the Saint's death day. It is so intricately inlaid and coloured that tears spring to his eyes. He has no need to read the dedication to know whose hand it is. 'I shall treasure it, treasure it', he mutters to Edmund in faraway Whithorn. How fine a craftsman! What a gift God has given him! He speaks the familiar words under his breath,

O God, thou hast cast us off, thou hast scattered us, thou hast been displeased; O turn thyself to us again.

Thou hast showed thy people hard things; thou hast made us to drink the wine of astonishment.

Indeed, he thinks, the wine of astonishment, and we shall drink deeper yet.

Although their journey from Whithorn had been easy, on good tracks and with a west wind behind them, it had seemed endless to Stitheard. Now he is in a fever of impatience to speak to Aedwulf – but whenever he calls on him, his servant turns him away.

'The Bishop is at prayer. He cannot speak with you now.'

When they sit at dinner, Aedwulf speaks generally to the company, with a tale or a homily for their instruction. The Whithorn brethren hang on his words, memorising his teaching to carry home with them. Stitheard can scarcely pay attention. It is clear, he thinks; I am hardly better than a heathen myself, after all these years.

When at last he enters the Bishop's room, Aedwulf bids him still himself.

'Why so urgent, my son? If what you hope for is God's will, He will bring it about.'

Stitheard stares at him. Aedwulf's tranquil stillness seems to belong to a different, unreachably distant world. He reaches for explanation but the words come tumbling out all together.

'I want to marry, Father. The girl is Norse, and if I do not return swiftly her father will marry her off to a heathen trader and I will lose her for ever.'

'Is this why you want to renounce your vows?'

'Yes, Father.'

Well, there it is. He has said it. There is no point trying to excuse or explain. Aedwulf is silent, and Stitheard cannot tell what he is thinking.

'What is the girl's name, Stitheard? What is her family?'

'Aase. Her father serves the Norse thane who has the land near the monastery. She has three brothers older than her.'

'They are heathen?'

'Yes, Father. But the Norse do not trouble the monks', he adds, half pleading. 'They are farmers like our own people.'

The Norse, thinks Aedwulf. Like our own people. This is how it happens, this is how peace comes. He turns his head aside to pray, his eyes half closed as he contemplates the Saint's will. Stitheard is caught into Aedwulf's silence and is still. Outside, he can hear a dog barking. His fears slip away.

At last, Aedwulf turns back to him.

'You have seen, my son, that in these dark times I have given leave to men to lay aside their vows if they have not the strength to hold them.' He pauses.

'Your case is different. You have been chosen to serve the Saint – and neither I, nor any man, can release you from that service.'

'I know it, Father. I do not seek to be released from his service. But I have not taken my final vows. I am still a novice. I can serve the Saint as a married man.'

Aedwulf gazes at Stitheard. His strong, young presence seems to fill the room. A short beard half covers his mouth now but his eyes betray all his restlessness and intensity.

'Let me marry, Father. I love her.'

'I cannot release you, Stitheard.'

There is a long silence. Stitheard closes his eyes to calm himself. An image comes to him of his vigil at Whithorn, of the long night beside the Saint. He opens his eyes again, finds Aedwulf's gaze upon him and speaks again.

'I swear the Saint does not oppose it, so long as I serve him still.'

His words hang in the air and he is astonished at his own boldness. Aedwulf is astonished too.

'The Saint does not oppose it? Are you certain that you know that?'

Stitheard hesitates, shocked at his own presumption. He remembers that he has felt like this before, in the shipmaster's hall. But this time he will speak.

'I am certain.'

Aedwulf turns away again. He is shaken by Stitheard's certainty. The boy has been close to the Saint for years now. It may be that he hears the Saint's will as surely as he does himself. He searches his own heart for the opposing certainty, but he does not find it. The silence is endless. At last he gives in. He gestures for Stitheard to kneel as he rises to his feet to deliver the judgement.

'Stitheard son of Hibald, I discharge you from your vows as a novice of the Order of St Benedict, as I will witness by my own hand. You will continue in the service of God as a lay brother. You are free to marry, but your wife must be baptised as a Christian. However, you are not released from your service to the Saint. You will be in his service till your death. If you have a son, the obligation will pass to him on your death. You should live close to wherever the shrine of the Saint may be, but you must work to support your wife and any children God is pleased to give you.'

He pauses. Stitheard moves forward and kisses his ring. His heart is alight with joy.

The Bishop blesses him, but an awkwardness has come between them. Stitheard wants to ask him, 'Am I still your son? Do you forgive me?', but he cannot form the words. He is on his feet and almost gone when Aedwulf calls him back.

'Has there been word at Whithorn from Abbot Eadred, my son?'

Stitheard turns.

'Yes, father. A messenger came to us from the shipmaster, Master Roderic. The Abbot fled to Derwentmouth after Alfred was defeated. He fell ill and was near to death, but God has spared him. When he is recovered he will join the brothers at Whithorn.'

'Thank God he is preserved.'

He had been sure that Eadred was there, somewhere, but he could not tell where. Even now. He feels a flood of relief. He turns his attention back to Stitheard, knowing they must be reconciled before he leaves.

'My dear son …', he begins.

He sighs and looks down for a moment, unable to continue. How he had loved the two boys, Stitheard and Alric, growing up together in the monastery on the Island. He had loved them as his own sons. Now Alric is lost to the rebels and Stitheard has renounced his vows. The grief he feels is as bitter as wormwood, but he submits himself. He will not oppose the Saint's will. It may be, he comforts himself, that the boy is his inheritor in ways he cannot understand. He holds his hand out to Stitheard and smiles at him.

'God bless you, my son, and my blessings on your marriage. I will write the judgement for Abbot Trumwin. It should be carried by one of your companions so there is no doubt it is from my hand.'

He pauses, considering.

'You will need a bride price if her father is to favour you. I will make arrangements before you leave.'

Hardly a month after Stitheard and the Whithorn brethren have left, the messenger comes with word from Eadred. Aedwulf recognises his strong, bold hand on the parchment as soon as the messenger takes it from his bag.

'Have you come from Whithorn?' he enquires of the man.

'From York, my lord.'

'From York? Is Abbot Eadred at York?

149

'Yes, my lord.'

Baffled, Aedwulf holds the parchment and tries to understand.

'Were you able to travel safely? It is long since we have had news from York.'

'The new king-to-be gave orders for guards to go with us till we had crossed the Tyne, and from there we have had no trouble.'

'The new king?'

The messenger looks at him patiently. Have they heard nothing up here? It is the talk of all the country.

'Ubbe Ragnarsson is dead, my lord, slain in battle by King Alfred's men. His kinsman Guthred is likely to be elected king of York. Saint Cuthbert himself guided Abbot Eadred to where Guthred was held as a slave, so the Abbot is in high favour now in York.'

Aedwulf feels giddy with bewilderment. He steadies himself against the fence post.

'I see. I will read the Abbot's letter. You will find food and drink within, my son.'

He turns inside. His legs feel feeble and he has to steady himself against the wall as he staggers to his room. He sinks onto the bench and unrolls the scroll.

'To Aedwulf, Bishop of Lindisfarne, beloved brother in Christ, greetings.'

He reads the letter, and then he rereads it; he gets up and paces the room; sits down and reads it again. At last he leans back, staring out of the door. He smiles, and then lifts his head as he laughs aloud.

25

AT THE HALL OF THE NORSEMEN

WHITHORN, DECEMBER 878

IT IS EARLY DECEMBER WHEN THE TRAVELLERS ARRIVE BACK AT WHITHORN. Although the trees are bare the countryside is still green. Stitheard breathes the soft westerly breeze, so different from the bracing air of the east. It makes him think of Aase.

At the monastery, all the brothers are eager to see them. Everyone wants to welcome them back, to get the news and to hear Aedwulf's teachings. Even more, they want to know the judgement. Stitheard has told his travel companions that he will give up his vows, but they are discreet. Everyone waits for Chapter.

On the morning after their return, Abbot Trumwin calls a Chapter meeting. He is a pious man, but rigid in his beliefs. He has read the judgement and his jaw is tight with disapproval. He does not look at Stitheard as he tells the brothers that the Bishop has sent a judgement on his petition. He reads aloud from the scroll. When he finishes, the air is charged with scandal. There is a long, long silence. At last Hunred says,

'Is this true, Stitheard? You are going to marry? – a heathen girl?'

'Yes.' He is sorry, for Hunred is a good man. He tried to help him and he had been deceived. But it was not his intention.

The silence deepens again. The Bishop's judgement hangs in the air, and no one wants to be the first to speak against it. At last the Abbot speaks.

'We grieve that you have renounced your vocation and must leave us, Stitheard. We fear that you have been led astray. However, we will

151

obey the Bishop's instructions. As he says here, you will continue to serve the Saint as a lay brother. You may attend monastic services. A hide of land belonging to the monastery will be given to you, as the Bishop has stipulated, but you will not be entitled to any further support from the monastery. From this day you must find lodging outwith this house.'

Stitheard understands. The Abbot is throwing him out. Well, he can survive, somehow. Nobody speaks. Then Edmund pulls himself upright to turn towards Trumwin. His face is lined from the pain he suffers from his shattered leg. It has made him an old man before his time, but his views are as forthright as ever.

'Father Trumwin, this is too harsh. It is not right that one of the Saint's bearers should be put out, and at the hardest time of the year. Nothing he has done can change what he is. Let him have lodging here till he can build a hut and sow his land.'

Stitheard is astonished. His heart lightens and he glances over to Edmund gratefully.

Trumwin turns red with annoyance. He glares at Edmund, displeased that so senior a brother should contradict him.

'There is nothing in the Bishop's instructions about providing lodging. He is now a lay brother, after all.'

'Lay or cleric, Father, he is still our brother.'

Trumwin turns to Hunred to support him. Hunred looks at his boots for some time, trying to make sense of his confusion. At last he speaks carefully.

'You are right, of course, Father Trumwin. However, we have heard in the judgement that Bishop Aedwulf has given his blessing to Stitheard's marriage. He says clearly that it does not prevent him from serving the Saint with us, his fellow bearers. Perhaps we should look upon this as an exceptional case, Abbot. These are not ordinary times.'

Stitheard sees Edmund, Leofric and Franco murmur together in agreement. He feels a shock of relief. They love him still. He scarcely hears the rest of the discussion.

At last Chapter is over. Abbot Trumwin and the Whithorn brothers file out, but the bearers linger. Stitheard makes for Edmund, embraces

152

him and asks his forgiveness, according to monastic custom. He turns to Leofric and sees in his face what he has not understood before – that some secret part of Leofric wishes himself in Stitheard's shoes. He embraces him.

'Forgive me, brother.'

Then Hunred and Franco are behind him and he must beg their forgiveness too, so that their brotherhood is restored. He is overwhelmed with joy. They stand close together, till a stool must be found for Edmund.

'Who is this girl?' asks Franco. 'When did you learn to speak Norse?'

'Has her father agreed? Does he know you're a monk?'

'What did Aedwulf say?'

Stitheard pretends to cover his ears.

'I'll tell everything. Whatever you want to know. But first, I have to go and find her.'

By the time he reaches the coast, the short December afternoon is already fading into dusk. For the first time, he follows the track to the Norse farmstead. He can see the outlines of the huts and the thane's hall. There are still one or two people moving around with lights so he stays at the edge of the trees. He can see the hill Aase told him of, at the far side of the farmstead. He makes his way through the trees till he is close. He can just make out a track and follows it to the spring.

Of course she is not there. How would she be, when darkness has fallen? Yet he feels a bitter shock of disappointment. He has lived for this moment for so many weeks. He slips back to the wood and cutting a stick, he sharpens the point. Then he rips a piece off his cloak, pierces the cloth with the stick and pushes it into the ground by the spring. Then he leans down and drinks for a long time, and fills his bottle. He turns away and makes his way back down the track, away from the huts and the hall, away from her. If she is still there, that is. If she has not been taken in a Norse trader's longship.

It is dark now and the moon has not yet risen. He retraces his steps and makes his way down to the coast, stumbling and slipping in the darkness. Once he is on the beach, he is sure-footed and finds his way to their shelter. It is still there. Dry leaves and bracken are piled on the floor. She has been using it, then. He sniffs, half certain he can smell her in the sweet decaying odour of the leaves. He takes a handful of leaves outside the shelter and makes a fire circle. His flint stones send a shower of sparks through the darkness and the leaves catch easily. He fetches wood and builds a good fire, glowing hot and yellow in the darkness. Pulling out his knife, he takes up a piece of elm and starts to whittle a little figure for her. A bird, it will be. Soon he is absorbed, whittling away the pale wood into the fire, his hands ruddy in the firelight.

When she finds him in the morning, he is curled up in his cloak in a nest of leaves and bracken. He opens his eyes as she squats down beside him. For a moment he is bewildered and stares at her as if she were a wood spirit. She is wearing a hood that covers her hair; her face looks pale in the brown woollen cloth, and her eyes are dark. Then in a moment he is awake.

'Aase!' he shouts, 'Aase!' And he jumps up from his bed of leaves, seizes her in his arms and embraces her so tightly that she gasps her breath out. Then he must kiss her, again and again, and swing her around and shout aloud. When he is calm she buries her head in his shoulder and leans against him. He feels a little sob come from her and looks down in surprise. He turns her face towards him and sees tears on her cheeks.

'I think you don't come back', she says. 'It's so long.'

He wipes the tears away gently with his fingers.

'I do come back.' He kisses her again. 'I come back for you.'

He feels in his tunic for the bird he has carved for her. She takes it up with a little cry of delight.

As the late sun rises they sit close together, warm with each other and Stitheard's cloak wrapped round them both.

'My mother knows.'

'Did you tell her?'

'She ask me … she ask me why I cry.'

He strokes her cheek, as if to wipe away forgotten tears.

'My mother helps us. She is glad that I stay close to her. But my father ….'

She makes a face.

'My father is very angry. He want to kill you.'

Stitheard pictures a belligerent Norseman waiting for him with a huge axe.

'I have silver, Aase. I can give him a bride price.'

'Is it much? He wants a rich man for me.'

'Tell him that the Saint protects me, and if you marry me he will protect you and all your family. Riches will come to him in a different way.'

She stares at him.

'Is it true?'

'It is true.'

Stitheard sees Aase's father for the first time when he is summoned to the Norse lord's hall. Garth is a thickset man with a chest like an ox. His hairy bristling eyebrows give him a lowering expression, and his lined face has an angry set. He rests his brawny arms on the table and glowers across the hall. Stitheard tries not to meet his gaze. It is enough to sit here in a hall full of the Norse folk without trying to deal with his father-in-law to be.

Although the entrance to the hall is carved with pagan figures painted in bright colours, inside it is not so different from Roderic's hall, or the hall at Elsdon. But the sound of all the heathen voices makes him feel utterly alone. Aase sits with her mother and the other women at the back of the hall, where he can hardly see her.

155

The uproar over the marriage has been brought to Garth's master, Lord Eigil. Although he sits at the head of the table, Eigil would be noticed in any company. He is very tall, with long brown hair falling to his shoulders. He is past middle age now, but he is still strikingly good looking, though his mouth is cruel. He wears a fur-trimmed cloak over his tunic and sits back in his chair watching over the hall. He drinks heavily but gives no sign of drunkenness. The talk is all in Norse and Stitheard must wait till later for Aase to tell him what was said. She does not tell him everything.

Eigil pushes his cup to one side and slaps the table with his hand for silence. Everyone looks at him expectantly.

'Well, Garth. Tell us your troubles.'

'Lord, look at this little weasel my daughter has brought in from the wood. He doesn't deserve to live, let alone marry my daughter. He has bewitched her with Saxon spells.'

Everyone stares at Stitheard. He stares back as boldly as he can. They see the strange light in his eyes, and recognise him at once as a sorcerer.

'Where has he come from? Is he a churl?'

'He says he was shipwrecked, Lord.'

'Ah', says Eigil. He has heard of this shipwreck. 'Is he one of those that brought the body of the Saxon holy man?'

'Aye, lord. He hangs around at the monastery. They are giving him some land to get rid of him. You can see he is good for nothing.'

Eigil favours Stitheard with a long appraising stare.

'Are you hasty, Garth? He looks strong enough to me.'

'But he is a Saxon, lord.'

'Is he a sorcerer?'

'For sure, lord, how else would he bewitch my daughter?'

Eigil leans back in his chair and picks at his belt, considering. He turns to his companions and they talk in low voices till he comes to a decision. He sits up and strikes once more on the table.

'I have heard that the relics of the Saxon holy man have power. If this man is a sorcerer, and if he is protected by the holy man, he could cause trouble. I don't want him casting spells on the hall. But a

156

marriage will make peace between us and the Saxons. Let the marriage happen.'

Garth turns red. Stitheard sees he is upset and feels a little spring of hope. Garth starts spluttering,

'But Lord, my daughter, look at her, Lord. She could make a good match, she could bring a fine price, she ....'

'Enough, Garth. You are a good steward to this hall. I will make a gift to you on the marriage.'

Garth bows his head and falls silent, though his face is swollen with rage. Eigil turns to look for Stitheard and beckons him over. Stitheard gets to his feet and goes to stand in the hall in front of him. Hands push him forward till he understands he must kneel. Eigil does not bother to stand but angles himself in his chair to get a good view of the Saxon. Yes, he thinks, there is a strangeness about him. It is unlucky for Garth but it is better to keep on the right side of the Saxons when you live in their midst. He summons his Saxon to his tongue.

'Saxon, I give you consent. You marry Aase, daughter of Garth. The bride price is fifty silver coins.'

There is a murmur from the hall.

'Now go.'

Eigil turns back to his drinking companions. Stitheard gets to his feet and bows. A couple of men clap him on the back and lead him from the hall.

Out in the daylight, he gasps for air. How can this have happened? What persuaded Eigil? It is certainly a miracle.

26
chester-le-street

york, may 879

EADRED STAYS WITH BISHOP WULFHERE IN YORK OVER THE WINTER, so that he can keep close to Guthred. He takes to overseeing Wulfhere's household. Wulfhere does not notice what he eats or keep account, and every servant in the place lives better than their master. Eadred sets about bringing order. A bishop should have a good table, at the very least. He watches the servants carefully till he finds a man he can bring on as his man servant. Beornric would not have wished him to be unattended, he tells himself, and if by a miracle Beornric should return, his position would be restored to him at once. Meanwhile, he eats very often at the King's hall. Guthred sends for him most days. Sometimes he must wait while Guthred recovers from a night of drinking and womanising, or when he goes hunting with his thanes. Eadred whiles away the morning enjoying the Dane's fine wine and bides his time. He is satisfied that he has Guthred's confidence and that the king-to-be means to honour his promises.

They start to work together on the treaty for the Saint's land, looking at maps, talking to Guthred's councillors, and haggling over details. It will be written in the Saxon language, so Eadred must act as secretary and Guthred's clerks must check the details, over and over. When Guthred tires of the negotiations, he sends away his clerks and calls for the tafl board.

'Will you play, Father?'

He has a passion for tafl, in all its forms. But Cyningtafl – King's Table – is his favourite and he will have Eadred play him till he has observed and learned all the Abbot's cunning and skill. He is no match for him yet but then he is still new to the game.

'Yes indeed, my lord. I hope I may be a worthy opponent.'

The serving men bring wine. The two men, the young Danish prince resplendent in gold and fine linen, and the distinguished Saxon churchman in his long robes, settle themselves companionably at the table. How strange is destiny, thinks Eadred, that he should find himself tafl tutor to a Ragnarsson – a Dane whose mind is yet as like to his as if he were his kin.

The tafl board is finely carved of polished elm wood, with the nineteen square chequers inlaid in light wood. Guthred takes up the two bags of taflstannas and broods for a moment. Then he looks up at Eadred, all charm.

'Why not take the king today, Father? Let us see if you can preserve him from my warriors.'

Eadred smiles his assent and takes up the smaller bag. He tips out his twenty-four dark men and their king. Each piece is a squat hemispherical warrior, carved from horn. The king stands higher than the other pieces, carved from wood and brightly painted. Guthred has forty-eight light men. He waits while Eadred positions the king in the centre of the board with his bodyguards about him, then tips out his pieces and arrays them round the edges of the board. Eadred's king must defeat the opposing warriors and manoeuvre his way to one of the four corners of the board. Here, only a king may sit.

'There, my lord – I am ready for you.'

'Indeed, father, my men are ready for you. I swear they will show you no mercy.'

Eadred moves the first of his pieces and the game begins.

Like all novices Guthred is eager for captures, though his early successes are easily undermined by the Abbot's seasoned tactics. Today, Eadred observes that he is trying a new strategy. Instead of bold sorties, he is bringing his army forward steadily, massing them closer and closer to the king. Eadred picks off a few of the front men but Guthred perseveres. Both men lean forward, intent, grey head and fair head close together.

'Ha! I think I have you, Father!'

'Not yet, my lord.'

Eadred slips his king away through a gap Guthred has not perceived. He will let Guthred have his prey, but not yet.

The game is long and there are few pieces left on the board when at last Guthred surrounds the king with a crow of triumph.

'I have you!'

'Well played, my lord, well played indeed. A new plan, if I am not mistaken?'

Guthred nods, delighted with his success. Both men sit back while Guthred calls for more wine, and the Abbot lets him savour his triumph for a while. After they have raised their cups to toast the victory, Eadred opens another conversation.

'I met with the messengers from East Anglia in your hall, my lord, from King Aethelstan.'

'Yes – Guthrum – we call him by his Danish name in York.'

'Indeed.' This was not a promising start but Eadred presses on. 'As you know, my lord, the king and all his thanes were baptised after the Peace of Wedmore. Would your lordship not follow his example, in brotherhood? The old gods are losing their hold on the people, and as a Christian king you would find alliances in the Saxon kingdoms and in Frankia.'

'King Guthrum and his thanes were defeated by Alfred. They had no choice but to convert. Here in the Kingdom of York the Danes are free to follow their own ways.'

'The Saint has favoured you with his protection beyond any other man. Do you not think, my lord, that he means to bring you and your people to salvation?'

'I know the Saint has helped me, father. I hold him in honour before any other god – pagan or Christian.'

Guthred is suddenly emotional and tears fill in his eyes. For a moment, Eadred sees again the raw youth he knew at Whittingham.

'He is my protector and I will be generous to him. You know this, father.'

Eadred nods. He holds his peace. Guthred gathers himself.

'But I will not convert. Already some of my thanes think I favour the church too much. The Kingdom of York is not a vassal of Alfred and his priests: it is a kingdom of the Danes, and I will be its king.'

Eadred retreats. The boy is not wrong, he thinks. And no one could doubt his loyalty to the Saint.

'You are just, my lord. We owe you nothing but gratitude for your generosity to the Saint.'

'Another game, father?'

But Eadred excuses himself – it is growing dark, he must return to say mass with the Bishop. After he has gone, Guthred sits alone for a long while, the painted king still in his hand.

When Spring comes, Guthred is crowned king in York with great ceremony. Bishop Wulfhere anoints him with the holy oil and blesses him in the name of the Trinity, and the Danes make sacrifices to Odin. The feasting and drinking go on for days, till there is not a sober man in the town, Dane or Saxon. Guthred gives gold and land to his thanes, drinks deep and womanises.

Once the celebrations are over, Eadred bids farewell to Bishop Wulfhere and makes preparations to journey north. Before he leaves, Guthred summons him to the King's Hall. When he arrives, the King is hearing a petition from a group of merchants in the town. They are wealthy men in rich fur cloaks and silk robes. The Danes have brought prosperity to York.

He finds Guthred seated in his tall chair, wearing a circlet of gold on his brow. His carefully combed fair hair has grown to his shoulders and there are more ornaments on his chest and arms. The dull shine of the gold is breathtaking. Eadred bows low before him. Serving men bring wine for him and platters with cakes and nuts. When the men are gone, Guthred comes down from his chair of office and sits at the table opposite Eadred.

'The town is full of merchants, Abbot. The people here are traders, not warriors. They want to grow rich. They think my taxes are too high!'

The remark is casual but Eadred understands from it that he wants to talk.

'It is always a problem, my Lord. They want good governance, but they don't want to pay for it.'

Guthred settles down easily. He tells him about the petition and probes a little for the Abbot's advice. When Eadred speaks, Guthred turns away, feigning inattention. Eadred is not disconcerted. He knows Guthred depends on him, but he does not wish this to be observed. When he is satisfied with Eadred's council he withdraws again into his authority.

'So, Father, you are travelling north. I will send horses and men to the Bishop's lodging.'

'You are generous, my lord.'

'You will talk to the Bishop of Lindisfarne about our plans.'

'Indeed, my lord. I believe he is overjoyed at the news.'

The courtesies concluded, they bid one another farewell. Eadred has leave to go north.

Guthred has seen to it that he is well mounted, and that the journey will be easy for him. The countryside is in the first bloom of early summer and Eadred feels his heart lighten. The trees are coming into leaf and cuckoos call in the meadows. He sees the green barley sprouting and men working the land. He tastes peace.

In his bag, he carries the treaty. Guthred has not disappointed him; indeed, the King has been generous beyond Eadred's hopes, and has won the consent of his council to the treaty. The Danish merchants and land holders were not slow to see the advantages. The Saint's land would separate their prosperous settlements in Deira from the rebels of Bernicia. No longer would Danish farmers live in dread of raiders firing their homesteads and stealing their crops. No armed men may cross the Saint's land to defile the sanctuary; no raiders, murderers or looters. For these Danes turned settlers, giving up their claim to Bernicia is a price worth paying.

When the terms were finally agreed, the Abbot and the King embraced formally in front of Guthred's council. The King presented him with a gold chain, intricately wrought. Eadred struggled to contain his pleasure in a formal bow. When he retired to his chamber he slipped the chain over his head and held it for a long time, letting the delicate links of gold run through his fingers from one hand to the other.

It is astonishing. It is glorious – miraculous even. The Saint himself is the blessed peacemaker and he will be venerated in Northumbria for ever. And somehow, he, Eadred, and a heathen slave cured of his fits, have been the means of bringing this about. Who could doubt the power of God and his saints? But, he soberly reminds himself, he still has to convince Earl Aelberht and the Northumbrians. God forbid that Aelberht should be as stubborn as his nephew.

First though, he has an important visit to make on his journey north. He and his companions travel the Roman road that runs east through Deira up to the bridge over the Tyne at Newcastle. A little to the west of the road, on a rise above the valley of the Wear, there is another relic of Roman times, a grey walled fortress built to keep watch over the road. There is no settlement near it now and the great stone walls stand alone. The wooden buildings inside have long since rotted away.

When Eadred and his companions arrive at the fort, it is already dusk. They ride through the stone entrance pillars, still high and imposing. Inside is rough, tussocky land with grass mounds where buildings once stood. On the flat land there are a couple of big fire circles with remains of blackened wood. There are animal pens in one corner and a makeshift shelter up against the walls. As Guthred had hinted to him, it is not completely deserted. He lets the reins drop as he stares around. His horse lowers his head and starts cropping the grass.

'What about water?' Eadred asks his companion. 'Is there a spring?'

They both look round. There is nothing obvious. But a fort like this, in Roman times, would not expect a siege.

'Perhaps there is a spring outside. Or maybe they used the river. It is not far.'

Eadred gazes round the space. He glances up at the sky to ascertain the orientation of the fort. It looks as if east would point directly to the river. He picks up the reins and urges the horse forward, to one of the fire circles. Paving stones are clearly visible under the ash.

'There was a building here. It must have been important – they would not have bothered putting paving in a barracks, surely.'

His companion shrugs, losing interest. The servants are getting bread and cheese out of the saddlebags and setting a fire. It is time to eat.

After they have eaten he walks outside, looking down over the valley to the river. The weather is fine and the sky is clear and full of stars. How tranquil it is!

They sleep that night in the fort, their bedding close to the walls, with the night sky in a great square above them. A crescent moon rises, pale between the dark clouds. It is a sign, surely, thinks Eadred.

The fort is Guthred's idea, of course. At first, it sounded like pure benevolence.

'The fort is yours, Abbot', Guthred told him, blue eyes wide open. 'The Roman name is Concangis. The folk call it Chester. It's on the Roman road, it will be easy for people to visit the shrine there. It is a fine spot near the river, and there is draught enough for ships to come upriver. And should there ever be trouble, your people will have protection within its walls.'

He had searched his memory for an image of the place. He vaguely remembered seeing the fort on a journey between York and Lindisfarne but that was many years ago. It sounded good, of course. But he was growing accustomed to Guthred's habit of calculation and wondered what had prompted this move. I have tutored him too well, he thought. Soon he will be a match for me. They play different parts now – Eadred as grateful supplicant, Guthred the open-handed king – but they both understand the game. Neither of them ever refer to Whittingham. As he had risen to leave, Guthred had stayed his arm.

'One more thing, Abbot, that I have forgotten to mention to you. About the fort. Our people are still troubled by the raiding parties from Bernicia. Once they have crossed the Tyne, they like to rest their horses for a night or two. My people tell me they use the fort.'

Aha, thinks Eadred to himself. Now we have it.

'The shrine, of course, will be a holy place. As we agreed, no arms will be carried in these lands.'

'No indeed, my lord, no indeed – a place of peace, they shall beat their swords into ploughshares, as the Holy Book has it.'

The reference had been too much for Guthred's Saxon, fluent as it was. But he was satisfied that they understood each other.

In the morning Eadred is up early, stalking like a gaunt old heron through the fort, hunched in his fur cloak against the dew-soaked chill from the ground. He sees where the shrine must be built, here, at the front of the site towards the river. He can make out the paving; for sure, it was the headquarters of the fort. It will be a wooden building to start with, but they can use the paving.

The domestic buildings can be set well back, he decides, there is room enough. The kitchen and bake-house will be at the far end, and the guest house too. There must be room for pilgrims. And a scriptorium. The Bishop has been insistent about the scriptorium. He is right, of course. The Word must be copied and preserved, after all the destruction. But surely Aedwulf will not try and persuade Edmund to come from Whithorn. We must send for Hunred, he thinks. There is so much to decide. Guthred will make the treaty known in the summer, if all is well, and we must be ready.

He walks out of the entrance, and follows a track down towards the river. He can see smoke rising through the trees and there are cattle grazing on the water meadows. There must be a settlement nearby. He stops on the rise and gazes down towards the river. It meanders in long loops through the valley, its waters full and flowing, the banks overhung with willow and alder. He watches the moorhens scuttling between the branches and a pair of swans slowly gliding downstream. How like it is to that other river, the river Eden flowing below his abbey, flowing still through his heart. A sharp pang of nostalgia grips him. It is so like Carlisle.

He turns away and looks back up to the fort. He pulls the beads from his belt and mutters a prayer. He should not be superstitious, he tells himself. The Lord is giving back what He has taken away, and with His help, it will be more glorious than before.

27

aelberht of bamburgh

bamburgh, june 879

IN ITS DAYS OF GREATNESS BAMBURGH WAS THE HOME of the kings of Northumbria, before the kingdom was divided and before the coming of the Danes. A steep outcrop of whinstone dominates the settlement, rearing high above a long sweep of pale sand and a wilderness of dunes and marram grass. Along its summit the kings built their palace looking out to sea, a fortress secure against the boldest attack.

A stone path curves round the south side of the cliff, and up this path ride four horsemen, reins slack as the horses labour on the slope. They reach a terrace below the entrance, and dismount. Eadred stamps and stretches as his men take the horses.

'I am become a fine horseman, Aedwulf. I will forget how to walk soon, after so much travelling.'

'Thank God for it, Eadred. My travelling days are done.'

'Does your back pain you?'

Aedwulf shrugs. The two men move forward on the terrace to stare out to sea to the Inner Farne looming from the water like a whale's back, and the other Farne islands fainter in the distance. They think of the Saint who made the Inner Farne his hermitage, and found his death there. A cold wind whips in from the sea, but they stand close to the terrace edge to catch a glimpse of the distant outline of Lindisfarne, dark against the morning blue of the sea.

'Is there anyone on the island?'

'It is said that two Danish families settled there, who farm the land. I don't know if they have stayed. The local people do not go there.'

Both men are silent for a while, watching the wind ruffle the waters. So much has changed, but not this.

Then the great wooden gates of the castle swing open and they walk through a half tunnel in the rock, into the fortress. Aedwulf staggers and Eadred calls his man to take his arm. They enter the Great Hall, lit with torches on the wall and with a fire in the hearth even on this bright morning. The casements are open but the light is dim coming in from the brightness outside. They blink and peer for a moment till they make out the men sitting at the table. Earl Aelberht is ready for them. Eadred bows low.

'Blessings upon the house, my lord Earl, and may God grant long life to you and your household. Bishop Aedwulf here accompanies me, my lord, and may I beg of your goodness a seat for his infirmity.'

Aelberht nods and there is a little bustle as Aedwulf and he are seated and ale is brought for them, and a hum of talk among the thanes. Eadred has leisure to watch Aelberht's face. He is past his first youth but strongly built with a high colour, and fair hair touched with grey at the temples. Will he be as intransigent as Ricsige? Well, much good it did him. Ricsige is dead now and all his intransigence is turned to dust.

When they are settled, Aelberht announces himself.

'Holy Fathers, you are welcome. I am Aelberht, Earl of Bamburgh and rightful king of Northumbria.' He glares round at his thanes as if daring them to refute it. 'I give you leave to speak.'

'Most noble earl and thanes, we are grateful indeed for your audience. I must set before you a proposal from Guthred, king of York.'

There is a rumbling and muttering from the benches, but Eadred presses on.

'You may have heard that Guthred, though he was kinsman to the Ragnarssons, was taken as a slave in his youth. After Ubbe's death, Saint Cuthbert visited me in a dream, unworthy though I am. The Saint bid me find the youth, and take him back to his people. He instructed me that I should support his election, and that Guthred would be the means of bringing him, Saint Cuthbert, home to his people.'

He takes a breath and glances at Aelberht's face. He is listening still. Eadred gathers himself.

'Now Guthred is king, he wishes to make a treaty, in gratitude to the Saint for his great favour. It is this that I seek to lay before you now.'

Aelberht nods for him to continue and Eadred begins to explain the treaty. As he speaks there is a gasp from the benches No one could have expected such an offer. All the land between the rivers Tyne and Wear!

'It is a bribe', growls Aelberht. 'He is using you, Abbot. He will give away some land to you, and then he will make you his watchdog so his settlers can sleep easy on their stolen land.'

'Indeed, Earl Aelberht, indeed, you are very right. Remember though, that the sword cuts both ways – or not, as in this case. The Danes cannot carry arms north either. You will be secure from attack. Although the Danes claim authority over all Northumbria, the land beyond the Tyne, all of Bernicia, will be yours in all but name.'

He sees Aelberht is trying to digest this. Eadred turns to the thanes.

'Noble lords, I beg you to heed this unworthy son of the church who has, nevertheless, received divine instruction through the person of our most holy Saint Cuthbert.'

They stare at him, bemused by his oratory.

'Be counselled by the Saint, my lords. He has chosen Guthred to be king of both Danes and Saxons and Guthred has in turn sought to show him honour in this treaty.'

'What of the lands in Deira, stolen by the Danes from our kinsmen? We have fought long and hard to win them back.'

'It is true, my lord, it is true. It is not an easy thing that is asked of you.'

Aelberht twists in his chair.

'Bishop Aedwulf, you have not spoken. Tell us your mind.'

Aedwulf is pale, worn out by pain from the arthritis in his back, and fatigued by the journey. He rallies himself but his voice can scarcely be heard.

'My son, heed Abbot Eadred's counsel. Guthred's treaty will bring peace to our people, and will honour the Saint.'

He sinks back into his seat. 'He is not well', thinks Eadred. 'I should not have persuaded him to come. But they must know that he favours it.'

Aelberht sees it too. He has known the Bishop since he was a boy and loves him as a father. He turns to Eadred.

'The Bishop is not well. He must rest, Abbot, and do you too. My thanes and I will speak in council.'

Eadred stands and bows. It is well enough for now, he thinks. He realises for the first time the Earl's love for Aedwulf and sees that his few words may carry weight where all his diplomacy would falter. He follows Aedwulf from the hall, with a final sweep of his robes.

The men take Aedwulf to an upper chamber and help him settle comfortably on a bench covered with furs. Serving women come and go with blankets and drinks and before long he is asleep.

'Will you eat, my lord Abbot?' the serving girl enquires.

'Later, I will eat later. I will stay now with the Bishop. Perhaps some wine, my good woman, could you do that? A jug of warmed wine?'

'Yes, my lord.'

Eadred settles himself comfortably in a chair beside Aedwulf. The room is warm enough from the heat of the great hall below. There is little daylight up here and candles have been lit for them. When his wine is brought he drinks contentedly. Not as fine as King Guthred's, of course, but a comfort after his meeting with the Earl. He ponders the council. Aelberht is full of bluster but he is not such a hothead as Ricsige was. He knows as well as anyone that the time for driving the Danes out of Deira is long past, but it suits him to send his young warriors down there – to burn out a Danish homestead or two and to remind the Danes that Earl Aelberht is still a force to be reckoned with. All that will have to stop. But in return, Guthred is giving up the Danish claim to Bernicia. Aelberht will be king of Bernicia in all but name. He must see it.

His thoughts wander to Alfred, who forced the defeated Guthrum to be baptised in Wessex and to take a Christian name. What is it? Aethelred? Aethelstan? Well, it saves confusion. Guthrum and Guthred. Guthrum king of East Anglia, Guthred king of York – it is confusing. Alfred has made a treaty with Aethelstan-Guthrum, making a boundary between Wessex and the Danelaw. This is how it must be. We cannot drive them out, but they cannot defeat us either. So we make boundaries, make peace, learn to live as neighbours. Ricsige would never have stomached it.

Is Alfred still sending messengers to Whithorn, he wonders. Well, he will not be able to add the Saint to his collection of relics. The Saint will be with his own people. Eadred allows himself to dwell on a vision of the land of the Saint's people, the holy land between Tyne and Wear, where they will build a great shrine to the Saint, here in the north where he belongs. God be praised, it seems that Guthred has been true to his word, Ragnarsson or no. Half dozing in the warm room, he dreams of a church like the great abbey church of Hexham, with its high clerestory and glorious coloured glass windows – but bigger, loftier, where the voices of boys singing like angels will float in the air. And he, Eadred, will be Abbot, in vestments of gold and silk, moving down the aisle with all the company of the folk ....

He wakes from his reverie and reproves himself for vanity.

'God forgive me', he mumbles to Aedwulf's sleeping form. At once the Bishop's eyes open, bright and piercing. He gazes at Eadred.

'God will forgive you all your sins, Eadred, for who has served him more truly than you? You will be blessed, brother, blessed ....'

He falls back to sleep. Eadred feels his eyes fill with tears as he gazes at his friend.

28

MASTER OF THE SCRIPTORIUM

NORHAM, JUNE 879

As THEY RETURN TO NORHAM, Eadred sees in the distance a man of medium height, stockily built, waiting for them outside the Bishop's house. Drawing closer, he sees the brown eyes and dark hair, now salted with grey, and with a little shock of recognition realises that it is Hunred, newly arrived from Whithorn. He feels a pang of remorse. It is three years now since the flight from Carlisle. Does he blame me still, he wonders. Does he blame me for my folly in ignoring Aedwulf's letter, in placing us all in such mortal danger? But Hunred greets him warmly with a smiling face. Eadred embraces him with relief.

'My dear brother, greetings to you, may God bless you.'

They help Aedwulf down from his horse, and follow him inside.

During the next few days the three men sit together in the Bishop's small chamber, the door and casement open to the mild summer air. Aedwulf has a chair lined with sheepskin at the head of the table while his two companions sit at either side of him. How pleasant it is to sit in this company, reflects Eadred. He and Aedwulf understand each other so well, but Hunred too is more open than in the old days. He used to be so resistant in his silent, stubborn way. Not now. In fact, he seems to hang on Eadred's every word.

For the first time Eadred realises that the story of his dream of the Saint has spread far and wide. Far from blaming him for his pride and folly, he sees that Hunred holds him now in great reverence. It makes him a little uneasy. Aedwulf, of course, understands the truth but to him, it is all equal. Whether it was a dream or an inspiration, it was from the Saint.

They talk of Whithorn and the other bearers, of Franco and his physic garden, Edmund and Leofric in the Scriptorium.

'What of Stitheard?' prompts Aedwulf.

'There is some difficulty, Father. Abbot Trumwin did not wholly accept the judgement.

'Ah. And you, Hunred?'

Hunred glances towards the Bishop.

'We do not doubt it is God's will.'

The Bishop nods.

'And the girl, Hunred? Is she baptised?'

'Yes, Father – she is baptised, and her mother with her.'

'And they are married?'

'Yes, Father.'

'There will be others, you know, like him. We must gather the brothers who have been scattered, to serve the new shrine. They have been living as laymen for years, with no thought of returning to their vocation. They may have taken wives also, may even have families.'

Hunred grapples with this, a little frown between his eyebrows.

'Father, will you … are you …?'

Aedwulf sees what is troubling him. Hunred was appointed head of the seven bearers and he has served the Saint faithfully; but he never sought authority and he longs now to return to his former life as an ordinary monk.

'Abbot Eadred will be Abbot of the new shrine at Chester-le-Street, my son. You will be at liberty from obligation.'

The frown disappears.

'But not yet, Aedwulf', says Eadred hastily. 'Not yet. We will need Hunred to be in charge of the building.'

Aedwulf is puzzled.

'My dear Aedwulf, the relics cannot stay at Chester-le-Street yet. There is nowhere suitable, no building yet within the fort. Until the shrine is ready, we will keep the relics elsewhere, and I will stay with them.'

'What are you planning, Eadred?'

'There is a small abbey at Crayke, a morning's journey from York, that has been spared destruction by the Danes. Bishop Wulfhere and I have visited the Abbot there, a very godly man. That abbey was given to Saint Cuthbert in the days of King Aldfrith and the Abbot desires nothing more than to welcome the Saint into his own. The relics will rest there while the shrine is built, and all the other necessary building.'

He will stay at Crayke while the build happens, Eadred has decided. It is near enough to York to allow him to keep Guthred's ear, and the guest quarters there are very comfortably appointed.

'I am not a practical man, my dear Aedwulf. It will be far better if Hunred is in charge, if he is willing. I will visit every week.'

Aedwulf turns towards Hunred. He nods resignedly.

It is dusk outside the hall and the serving men bring lights. They are growing weary but they have one more matter to settle. Eadred glances at Aedwulf to see if he needs to rest, but he nods for Eadred to continue.

'My son, it is the Bishop's wish to establish a scriptorium at the shrine. He would like our brother Edmund to be the master.'

'God knows best, Father, but I do not think Edmund can leave Whithorn. His leg was crippled in the shipwreck and it pains him a great deal to walk, even to stand. It has weakened him and he often takes a low fever. The scriptorium at Whithorn is well established now, and he has taught many of the brethren there.'

'What about Leofric?'

'He is like a son to Edmund. He cares for him – Edmund cannot walk without him. He is a good scribe, father, but I do not know if he should be a master.'

Eadred is surprised. This is a strong judgement for Hunred. However, he understands it well enough. No one works harder than Leofric but he does not have a natural talent, nor does he have an easy way with his brothers.

'What of the other brothers – the Whithorn brothers? Is there one of them who has learned enough, who could ….'

Aedwulf interrupts them.

'Let Stitheard be the master. He will do very well.'

They both stare at him, astonished.

'Stitheard has a fine hand', he says. 'He and Alric were taught by Edmund as boys in the scriptorium at Lindisfarne. I know his work.'

'But Aedwulf, he is only a lay brother now. He must work his land.'

'He is the servant of the Saint, Eadred, before any other duty. Until it is time for them to leave Whithorn, he must work in the scriptorium with Edmund, so that Edmund can prepare him. He must be supported by the monastery. I will write to Abbot Trumwin.'

Eadred gives up the argument. Usually Aedwulf yields to his judgement on all points, agrees with whatever he proposes. But every now and then, he makes his mind up on something unexpected, and Eadred no longer argues. For himself, he would never have considered Stitheard. His behaviour is, to say the least, unreliable – though certainly, he reminds himself, he has not wavered from his duty to the Saint.

'As you think best, Aedwulf', he concludes.

29

The Deed

York, 880

THE KING'S HALL IN YORK IS FULL. King Guthred himself sits at the high table with his thanes and earls on one side and Abbot Eadred, Bishop Wulfhere and the clergy on the other. King Alfred of Wessex has sent emissaries and gifts, for he is certain that his dream of the Saint led to his victory at Ethandun. Sallow Oswin, clerk to King Alfred, and his brethren sit uneasily next to Abbot Eadred. Earl Aelberht has not attended in person, but he has sent a company of his thanes to give his assent to the treaty.

The parchment is unrolled on the table before the king and the holy folk. King Guthred, resplendent in gold crown and silk robes, signals to the clerk to read the deed aloud.

*King Guthred's deed to the Haliwerfolc**

This is the deed which Guthred King of York has made to the Haliwerfolc for themselves and for their descendants, as well for born as for unborn, who reck of God's mercy or of his.

1. Concerning the land boundaries: along the river Tyne from the meetings of south and north rivers by Hexham, to South Shields and Jarrow, and along the river Wear from the river head to the river mouth at the sea, and including the estate of Chester and all its lands, and along Dere Street to the east.

2. Then is this: that the rents of all the lands are in use and custom of the Haliwerfolc as they shall determine.

3. And the King of York will levy no tax on either thane or churl residing on this land.

* People of the holy man.

4. Then is this: If a man be slain on these lands, we estimate all equally dear, Saxon and Danish, at eight half marks of pure gold; except for churls who reside on rented land and their freedmen; they also are equally dear, either at a hundred shillings.

5. And if a king's thane be accused of manslaying on these lands, if he dare clear himself on oath, let him do that with twelve king's thanes. If any one accuse that man who is of less degree than the king's thane, let him clear himself with eleven of his equals and with one king's thane. And so in every suit which may be more than four shillings. And if he dare not, let him pay for it threefold, as it may be valued.

5. And Guthred King of York has ordained this deed on sworn oath, that these lands shall be the possession of the Haliwerfolc, and both Dane and Saxon have sworn to carry no arms in these lands.

Abbot Eadred rises, a great bible in his hands. He holds it before the King, who places his hand upon it and speaks his oath, first in Danish, then in Saxon. There is a roar of applause from the crowded hall. For a moment, Guthred's eyes meet the Abbot's in a moment of complicity. 'You see?' say Guthred's eyes. 'I have done it.' The Abbot bows deeply before him.

Then the king takes up the quill and puts his mark on the parchment; his clerks melt the red wax and he stamps his seal upon it. The abbot and bishop kneel before him and receive the parchment and give it to their clerics to be taken to Crayke for safekeeping. The serving men run into the hall with ale and mead, with meat and fine foods of every kind. There will be a great feast in the hall, with Danes and Saxons too. Eadred turns to Wulfhere and embraces him. Then he gives orders to his man who leaves the hall and runs to the three men waiting by their horses outside. Their saddlebags are loaded for a journey. When they see Eadred's man, all he has to do is nod. They swing up into their saddles and clatter off down the street. They will be in Whithorn in a fortnight or less, and the Saint's journey home will begin.

30

ΑFTERWORD

chester-le-street, october 881

Those seven who were privileged to bestow more close and constant attendance upon the holy body ... had conveyed the body of the holy confessor from the island of Lindisfarne and had resolved that as long as they lived they would never abandon it.

Four of them, named Hunred, Stitheard, Edmund and Franco, were of greater repute than the other three; and it is the boast of many persons in the province of the Northumbrians, as well clerks as laymen, that they are descended from one of these families; for they pride themselves upon the faithful service which their ancestors rendered to Saint Cuthbert.

Simeon's 'History', Chap. XXVII

KING GUTHRED HAS SENT WORD TO CHESTER-LE-STREET THAT HE WILL VISIT. He wishes to see the progress of the Saint's shrine. He also wishes to take counsel with Abbot Eadred who has been residing at Chester-le-Street since the summer.

Since the news came, there has been a rush of activity to prepare for the king's visit. Franco is in charge of the guest house and has had to leave his physic garden alone while he organises preparations for the feast in the King's honour. Hunred is hoarse from shouting at the men who are finishing the roof of the shrine building. The scriptorium is swept clean and Aase has insisted on a new tunic for Stitheard. She and young Beric are waiting with the rest of the folk by the gate. Now the three of them – Franco, Hunred and Stitheard – stand with the Abbot inside the gatehouse of the fort, eager for their first glimpse of the king.

The Abbot's man is upstairs on the lookout for the royal party. It is a cold, raw morning with an early frost still on the ground. As soon as he sees the horses trotting along the old Roman road, he runs down the steps and gives word of their approach to his master. The Abbot clasps his fur-lined cloak around him, pulling its hood over his head and nodding to his companions to follow him out to the gate.

King Guthred rides at the front with his bodyguards around and behind him. He is magnificent in a polished leather tunic with studded silver tracework, a purple undertunic, and a deep scarlet fur-trimmed cloak half covering the sides of his black horse. He has a flowing fair moustache and long curling hair to his shoulders, held back from his face with a simple half helmet of silver. He is every inch a king of the Danes, commanding and majestic. His bodyguards are fearsome, tall warriors with shields hanging from their saddles, though their weapons have been left outside the sanctuary. At the rear are packhorses, loaded with the King's gifts for the shrine. All the folk and brothers line the road and gape in amazement at them.

The King swings down from his saddle and comes forward to greet the Abbot. They embrace formally, and servants run forward with cups of hot wine for the royal party.

'Greetings, my lord, and may God and his saints protect you.'

'Greetings, father.'

Guthred releases the Abbot and is presented to his three companions. He looks about him at the activity in the fort. Some buildings are already completed but there are still piles of wood and thatch straw everywhere. Everyone draws close to stare at the King and the Abbot waves them back to their work.

'Will you take refreshment, my lord?'

'No. Not yet. For my men though.'

He turns round and shouts an order to his bodyguard. They dismount and stand impassive beside their horses. Two follow close behind him.

'Show me round, Father. Let me see what you have been up to.'

Eadred and Hunred take him to the wooden church – roofed

179

now and nearing completion – that will house the relics. It is a small, simple building close to the east wall of the fort. It will serve for the present. Guthred pays close attention to what Hunred tells him, and sees where the Saint will lie. He turns to the Abbot to tell him about the gifts he has brought to adorn the shrine and both men bow in gratitude. When they move on to the monastery buildings and the scriptorium, Guthred quickly loses interest. He is not a lettered man. He puts a hand on Eadred's shoulder.

'Let us walk down to the river, Father. I want to talk to you.'

They take the path down the slope to the river. The willow trees overhanging the river are turning yellow and the fallen leaves drift down the river on the current. The Abbot draws his cloak more closely around him but the King gives no sign of feeling the chill of the day. He signs to his men to drop back. Eadred and he walk on ahead, side by side, out of earshot.

'You are often at Chester-le-Street these past months, father. I must come riding up the road to find you.'

'Indeed my lord, I beg your forgiveness. We still lack a prior, and there is much to attend to.'

'When will the Saint's relics be brought here?'

'In the spring, my lord, if God wills.'

'In the spring', Guthred muses. He stands at the river bank, watching the flow of the current.

'Crayke is a morning's ride but once you are up here I will never see you.'

He pauses and looks directly at Eadred.

'I need you, father. I have no one to beat me at tafl and my counsellors are slow-witted.'

'My lord, if God wills, once all is in order, I may attend on you in York more regularly.'

Guthred shakes his head.

'I have a better plan, father.' The blue eyes open wide in the old way and Eadred feels a shiver of amusement and apprehension.

'Wulfhere is an old man, father. He will not see the winter through. You must be the new Bishop of York, Eadred.'

180

He turns and takes Eadred's hands. He looks intently at him, to see what he makes of this move. He repeats, 'You must be the Bishop, father.'

'My son ....'

Eadred is lost for words. Guthred has outplayed him, for he has not seen this possibility.

All at once, he longs to leave Chester-le-Street with its cold muddy huts and ignorant, untrained men, and the whole tremendous effort of bringing the monastery and shrine into being. He will go to York and wear the Bishop's purple, he will sit by the King as his chief councillor with a gold chain of office, and live like a lord in the Bishop's hall.

'Yes! It is agreed then, Father?' Guthred has watched his face and is triumphant.

'Alas, my son, what could rejoice me more? I would sooner be of service to your lordship than any man living. But I am sworn to the Saint, my lord. I cannot leave him.'

'Is not the Saint my protector? Would he not want you to be Bishop in York, and my councillor?'

'But the shrine, my lord – the shrine.'

'Well, father – I will not push you for an answer now. Consider it and come and spend the Christmas feast with me. I will promise you a good table.'

They clasp hands upon it. Then they turn to go, Guthred giving Eadred his arm to help him up the hill, back to the feast that awaits them.

Stitheard rubs his chapped hands together and blows on them. It is too cold to work now and he has sent his pupils away. Aase will have hot food for him and Beric will be waiting for Daddy to toss him up in the air and rub his nose. But he has been held up with all the excitement of the King's visit and he wants to finish the manuscript he is working on. There is only a line of decoration to complete, and the colours are already mixed. They will go to waste if they are not

181

used. He bends over the parchment again, dips the quill, and starts the delicate line of colour inside the curving pattern.

He is almost finished when a man comes through the door, blocking his light. He looks up with a flash of annoyance and gestures the man to the side. He is a tall man with his cloak bundled around him. Stitheard cannot see his face clearly though as he enters the workshop he notices a long scar down his left cheek. What does he want, he wonders irritably. Since work started on the shrine, men have started to arrive from all over the kingdom and half of them would rather be scribes than builders.

'Please wait. I will talk to you when I have finished.'

He returns to his work and is absorbed again in a moment. When he finishes, he realises the man is almost behind him. To his astonishment, the man swings his legs over the bench and sits beside him.

'So where have we got to?' the man asks.

Stitheard swivels round to look at this impudent stranger. He sees the long scar, the grave eyes, the half-smiling mouth. He drops his quill.

'Alric', he says, opening his arms.

hiscorical noces

Bishop Wulfhere died in 892, but the see of York remained vacant for several years.

King Guthred died while still a young man, in 895. He was buried in a Christian ceremony at York Minster.

There are differing accounts of the date of **Bishop Aedwulf's** death, from 894 to 900. It is not known if he remained at Norham for the remainder of his bishopric, or if he moved to Chester-le-Street.

The date of **Abbot Eadred's** death is not recorded.

che scory

The story is based on the first known record of the bearers' journey. It was written in 1096, more than two hundred years later, by a monk, Simeon of Durham. As there are few written records from the period of the Danish invasion, Simeon's account is likely to be based on monastic oral traditions. The story forms part of his 'History of the Church of Durham', a record of the fortunes and migrations of the monks of Saint Cuthbert.

Simeon's account tells us of the widespread destruction in Northumbria following Ricsige's rebellion, of the flight from Lindisfarne, and the subsequent wanderings and adventures of the monks. Other historical and archaeological records enable one to establish a date outline for the rebellion and the destruction of monasteries and churches, for example at Tynemouth, Hexham and Carlisle. The story of Wessex and Alfred's struggles against the Danes in the same period are well documented, as is Alfred's veneration of Saint Cuthbert. The treaty with Guthred is also a matter of historical fact. It formed the basis for the County

184

Palatine of Durham, sometimes known as the Liberty of the Haliwerfolc. It survived as an autonomous county under the Prince Bishops until the nineteenth century.

However, the detail and chronology of the bearers' journey is difficult to establish from Simeon's narrative, and it has been the subject of much speculation. This account is a creative reconstruction of what might have happened that makes no claims for historical accuracy.

The body of Saint Cuthbert was moved to its final resting place at Durham in 995, after further incursions from the Danes. The cult of Saint Cuthbert continued to grow in importance throughout the Middle Ages, until the shrine was destroyed at the Reformation. To this day, however, his tomb remains behind the high altar in Durham Cathedral. The Lindisfarne Gospels are preserved in the British Library.

timeline

Saint Cuthbert and his cult

687   Death of Cuthbert, 20 March

710–720   Lindisfarne Gospels written and illuminated by Eadfrith

721   'Life of Cuthbert' by the Venerable Bede completed

The Vikings

793   First Viking raid on Anglo-Saxon lands at Lindisfarne

The Danish Invasion

866   The Great Army of the Danes arrives in Northumbria, led by the Ragnarssons

867   Battle of York, 21 March; Northumbria defeated and King Aella killed; Danes make York (Yorvik) their capital

868   Danes take Nottingham; Mercia under Danish control

869   King Edmund of East Anglia martyred; East Anglia under Danish control

870   All Saxon kingdoms except Wessex under Danish control

871   Alfred crowned king of Wessex

872   Revolt in Northumbria: Earl Ricsige claims the throne

874   Halfden Ragnarsson takes Danish army north to subdue the revolt

875	Tynemouth sacked; Lindisfarne abandoned	St Cuthbert relics taken to Carlisle
876	Hexham sacked	
877: March	Carlisle sacked	St Cuthbert relics taken to Crossthwaite in Cumbria
877: June		King Alfred offers sanctuary in Wessex for the relics
877: Nov	Famine in Cumbria	
878: January	Alfred defeated at Chippenham at New Year; takes refuge in the marshes of Athelney	St Cuthbert relics embarked for Ireland; shipwrecked at Whithorn
878: April	Ubbe Ragnarsson killed at battle of Cynuit	
878: May	Alfred victorious at Ethandun	In a dream, St Cuthbert directs Alfred to fight the Danes and assures him of his protection
878: July	Guthred the slave brought to York	In a dream, St Cuthbert directs Bishop Eadred to find a Danish slave who is to be King of York
879	Guthred elected King of York	
880	Treaty with St Cuthbert's people	St Cuthbert relics leave Whithorn
881	Construction of shrine and abbey at Chester-le-Street	St Cuthbert relics taken to Crayke
882	Chester-le-Street shrine consecrated	St Cuthbert relics installed at Chester-le-Street
995	Shrine moved to Durham	
1096	Symeon's 'History of the Church of Durham'	

about the author

Katharine Tiernan grew up in north Northumberland not far from Lindisfarne. After a sojourn in the heathen lands of the south, she now lives and writes in Berwick-upon-Tweed.